"I, good samaritan that I am, saved you from the ravages of the storm this morning. You owe me, Blaze Holland."

"Bill me."

"I will pick you up tomorrow night at eight for dinner."

"You will not."

"You're not getting out of this room until you agree," Taylor threatened.

"This is like a bad movie," Blaze muttered. "Oh, all right. But I hope you like talking to yourself because I don't intend to speak to you the entire evening."

Suddenly Taylor cupped her face in his hands and kissed her gently on the lips. In the next instant he pulled her tightly into his arms and deepened the kiss. Blaze's knees began to tremble. Somewhere in the back of her mind she wondered where her hands were, and her eyes flew open in horror as she realized they were tangled in Taylor's thick, dark hair, urging him closer.

"Until tomorrow night," he whispered huskily . . .

WHAT ARE *LOVESWEPT* ROMANCES?

They are stories of true romance and touching emotion. We believe those two very important ingredients are constants in our highly sensual and very believable stories in the *LOVESWEPT* line. Our goal is to give you, the reader, stories of consistently high quality that may sometimes make you laugh, sometimes make you cry, but are always fresh and creative and contain many delightful surprises within their pages.

Most romance fans read an enormous number of books. Those they truly love, they keep. Others may be traded with friends and soon forgotten. We hope that each *LOVESWEPT* romance will be a treasure—a "keeper." We will always try to publish

*LOVE STORIES YOU'LL NEVER FORGET
BY AUTHORS YOU'LL ALWAYS REMEMBER*

The Editors

LOVESWEPT • 61

Joan Elliott Pickart
Breaking All The Rules

BANTAM BOOKS
TORONTO · NEW YORK · LONDON · SYDNEY · AUCKLAND

BREAKING ALL THE RULES
A Bantam Book / September 1984

*LOVESWEPT and the wave device are trademarks of
Bantam Books, Inc.*

All rights reserved.
Copyright © 1984 by Joan Elliott Pickart.
Cover art copyright © 1984 by Susanna Steig.
*This book may not be reproduced in whole or in part, by
mimeograph or any other means, without permission.*
For information address: Bantam Books, Inc.

ISBN 0-553-21667-8

Published simultaneously in the United States and Canada

---

*Bantam Books are published by Bantam Books, Inc. Its trade-
mark, consisting of the words "Bantam Books" and the por-
trayal of a rooster, is Registered in U.S. Patent and Trademark
Office and in other countries. Marca Registrada. Bantam
Books, Inc., 666 Fifth Avenue, New York, New York 10103.*

PRINTED IN THE UNITED STATES OF AMERICA

O   0 9 8 7 6 5 4 3 2

For Scott—my love, my life, my friend.

One

"Oh, no," Blaze moaned as the lights dimmed, flickered once, and went out, enveloping the room in pitch-black silence. "Not now!"

Groping her way to the window, she opened the louvered shutters and looked down twelve floors to Fifth Avenue. The usual steady glow from the busy New York City street was obscured and the only light on this ghostly, snowy January night came eerily from the already congesting traffic. Moving cautiously, Blaze worked her way to her large desk and pulled open the middle drawer. She rummaged through pens, pencils, paper clips, and other sundry debris until her hand came to rest on a book of matches. Striking one, she walked slowly out of the bedroom and across the hall into the spacious living room, then quickly blew out the flame before it singed her fingers. Striking another, she lit the candle in the crystal hurricane lamp on the end table. Shadows danced across the walls in a warm, romantic glow, but Blaze was in no mood to appreciate the atmosphere.

"I can't believe this!" she said, sinking onto the soft beige sofa. She stared up at the ceiling, which she assumed was still there although she couldn't see it. "Why me, I ask you?"

She reached for the brown, trim-line telephone and dialed the number of the security desk in the lobby of the apartment building. The man on duty answered cheerfully.

"This is Blaze Holland in twelve-twenty-one. Do you have any information on this blackout?"

"Hello, Miss Holland. Sure is dark, isn't it? No way to know how long we'll be out, but you're not to worry because we have emergency generators and you'll have plenty of heat."

"I don't care about that, it's electricity I need."

"Sorry, but there's nothing we can do. There's a mean snowstorm blowing out there. It's a miracle the phone lines are still—"

"Hello? Hello?" Blaze dropped the receiver in disgust. Well, so much for the phones, she thought. No electricity, which meant no typewriter, which meant she'd never make her deadline, which meant . . . "Oh, hell," she said aloud.

She leaned forward, cupping her chin in her hands and resting her elbows on her knees, and scowled. It was nearly midnight, and she had planned on working through the night on the rough draft for the last chapter of the book so Murphy could type the final copy in the morning, but . . .

Getting up from the sofa, she stretched her long, slender body, then picked up the hurricane lamp and walked down the hall. There was no point in sitting up stewing over the situation she decided gloomily. Might as well go to bed. Having no penchant toward suicide she dismissed the idea of a shower in the dark and quickly stripped off her flannel shirt and jeans and put on a New York Jets football jersey.

It was her own fault, she fumed, blowing out the candle and settling into her king-size bed. She had known she was cutting it close when she'd taken Tilly to Las Vegas, but she had been sure there was still time. She should have asked Tilly to postpone the trip, but she had promised and Tilly had been saving nickels in a gallon jug for over a year. Of course, Blaze had never dreamed Tilly would insist on carrying the jug right onto the plane. It had weighed a ton, but Tilly was sure it would be bad luck to cash the nickels in for traveler's checks. They were her Las Vegas nickels, by gosh, and they were going with her!

Blaze laughed aloud. She would never forget marching into The Dunes in Las Vegas, a bellhop lugging the heavy jug, and setting Tilly up on a stool in front of a slot machine, the trusty nickels on another stool right beside her. Blaze had wandered around the dazzling casino, enjoying the exciting, sparkling atmosphere. She had checked on Tilly often, only to be waved away and told not to break the streak of luck the older woman was having. Blaze had attended a midnight show and then finally insisted that Tilly, at sixty-seven years old, must have a good night's sleep. The next morning Tilly had awakened Blaze at six, insisting time was wasting, and the ritual had been repeated for three more days.

A thoroughly exhausted Blaze and a sparkling Tilly had arrived back in New York, Tilly carrying her clothes in a grocery bag so that her suitcase could accommodate the nickels she had multiplied threefold. "She's crazy and I love her," Blaze said to the dark, empty room, "but right now those three days look awfully long. Oh, New York, how could you do this to me? I'm a nice person. I never jaywalk or mug people.

All I'm asking for is a little electric juice for my type-writer. Damn." She punched her pillow and lay back, only to toss and turn for more than an hour before falling at last into a restless slumber.

She was usually a light sleeper, so the noise of the downstairs buzzer woke her early the next morning. She was instantly up and dashing to the intercom. "Yes?"

"Miss Murphy is here, Miss Holland," the security guard announced.

"Send her up, please."

Blaze smiled when she noticed that the lights were burning brightly throughout the room and she quickly turned them off. The hum of the typewriter was music to her ears when she entered her work-room, and she patted the machine fondly as she shut it off. She was in the kitchen making coffee when a shivering Murphy arrived, begging for a cup.

"It'll be ready in a flash," Blaze said. "Is it really awful outside?"

"Grim," Murphy said, rubbing her hands together. "I'm too old for this stuff. Even my layer of fat didn't keep me warm."

"Right." Blaze laughed. "At thirty-six you really should start thinking about retiring to Florida to defrost your bones. And, for the fiftieth time, you're not fat, you're curvy. Nicely rounded."

"Didn't your Indian ancestors have some code against lying?"

"I don't know. Ask General Custer. Listen, Murphy." Blaze frowned. "We have a problem."

"Don't tell me, let me guess. You didn't get the rough draft done from your scribblings because of the blackout."

"You've got it."

"Great. Now what? We're running out of time here."

"I know, but I have a plan," Blaze said as she poured them each a mug of coffee.

"I'm all ears," Murphy said, sitting down opposite her at the table.

"Well, you stay here and finish the chapter you're working on. I'll go down to the library on Forty-second Street and type the rough draft for the last chapter and bring it back to you. Good, huh?"

"Fine, except there's a blizzard raging out there. Getting a taxi takes an Act of Congress."

"I'll throw myself under the wheels of a cab and beg to be taken to the library. I'd better get dressed and hit the road."

"You know I love that jersey, Blaze. I sure wish you'd tell me how you talked that football player into giving it to you."

"Who said I talked, my dear," Blaze said, batting her eyelashes.

"I bet you threatened to cast an ancient Indian spell over him that would turn his muscles into mush."

"Oh, at least." Blaze laughed as she left the room.

Three hours later Blaze pulled the last sheet of paper out of the typewriter and with a contented sigh placed it on the stack beside the machine. She had walked out of the front door of the apartment building and right into a taxi that was just letting out a fare. There were plenty of available typewriters at the New York Public Library. Now she was at last finished with the final chapter of the book. When she got back to the apartment she would proofread what Murphy had typed that morning while Murphy typed this chapter. Everything would be under control.

She hurried to the doors of the library and rushed outside, only to gasp and rapidly retrace her steps to the sanctuary of the building. It was sleeting, and with a groan Blaze realized that in her haste she had brought nothing with her to protect the loose typed pages she was hugging against her breasts.

Turning, she walked briskly into the ladies' room and pulled off her coat and the cardigan sweater she wore over a thick turtleneck. Wrapping the papers in the cardigan, she tied the sleeves in a knot and buttoned the bundle inside her coat.

"I look like I'm smuggling a bowling ball," she said, laughing at her reflection. She cupped her hands under her protruding stomach to insure that her precious cargo wouldn't drop. "Heavens, I can't even see my feet." She leaned over and peered down to where she knew her leather boots were supposed to be.

Outside, the biting snow whipped painfully against her face, and she squinted her eyes as she walked to the curb, hoping to catch sight of an available taxi. Suddenly she slipped on a patch of slush and shrieked as she felt herself losing her footing. Just as quickly she was upright again, strong hands gripping her arms tightly and setting her squarely on her feet.

"Are you all right?" a deep voice asked.

"What? Oh, yes, I'm fine. I . . ." He was gorgeous, she thought wildly, taking in the thick black hair, steel-gray eyes, tanned face, and shoulders wide enough to match the owner of her football jersey. "Thank you very much for stopping my fall."

"I wouldn't think you'd be out in weather like this in your . . . condition." The man frowned, his dark brows drawing together as he scowled at her.

"My what?"

"Your . . . you know." He waved a hand in the direction of her bulging midriff.

He thought she was pregnant! Blaze choked on a laugh and it came out in the form of a hiccup. "Oh, yes, my condition." She nodded solemnly. "Well, I'll just grab a taxi and hurry my little self right on home."

"That's not going to be so easy. Everyone wants a cab today. Look, why don't you let me give you a lift? My car is right around the corner."

"Oh, I don't think so." She wanted to, but it would be crazy to ride with a stranger, she thought, staring up at the handsome man, estimating him to be at least six-feet-four.

"Hey, I know this is New York and nobody trusts anyone, but I'll give you my mother's phone number and she can tell you I'm a decent guy. How's that?" He smiled, white teeth flashing and tiny laugh lines crinkling by his beautiful gray eyes.

"What do mothers know," Blaze muttered, and then shivered as the icy water invaded her coat.

"You're going to catch pneumonia. You'd better come with me right now. It's not just yourself you have to worry about, you know."

"Huh? Oh, yes, my . . . condition." She glanced down. "Well, all right. I'm just up on Fifty-ninth Street across from Central Park. I really do appreciate this." Blaze smiled as the man gently took her elbow and escorted her along the sidewalk. "Maybe you'd better tell me your name so at least I'll feel as though we've been introduced."

"Taylor Shay."

"Well, Mr. Shay, you've saved a lady in distress."

"My pleasure, Mrs. . . ."

"Miss."

"Oh. I just assumed that you were married because you're . . . well, it's none of my business, Miss . . ."

"Blaze Holland."

"Blaze? That's unusual. I like it."

"It's Indian. My grandmother was an Apache. I was named after her."

"Ah, that accounts for your silky black hair, big

dark eyes, lovely high cheekbones, and that glowing complexion. I've always thought the Indians were a very handsome people. Here's the car," he said, opening the door to a large, plush automobile. "Watch your step."

"Thank you," Blaze said, hastily shifting her drooping package while Taylor walked around to his side of the car and slid behind the wheel.

He started the engine, then turned to watch for an opening in the surging traffic, giving Blaze the chance to scrutinize him. His hair, like hers, was wet. The strong, large hands gripping the steering wheel had closely trimmed nails and a large signet ring that looked like a class ring. Even though he was wearing a heavy black overcoat, Blaze got the impression there was no excess weight on his tall frame. His face was finely chiseled, lips soft and sensuous, and those eyes . . . gray as a winter's day and framed by thick eyelashes as dark as his hair and brows.

Each feature taken individually, he was almost pretty, Blaze mused, but put them together and he oozed masculinity. She wondered where he had gotten that gorgeous tan in the dead of winter? Well, only one way to find out. "I can't help noticing your tan, Mr. Shay," she said pleasantly. "Have you been on vacation?"

"Skiing. Aspen," he said, still unable to move the car into the bustling traffic.

"That must have been fun."

"Yes, we had a great time."

We? We who? Mrs. Shay and the six little Shays? "Your whole family skis?" she asked.

"Family? No, my mother, who was going to give you a reference for my sterling character, is a little old for the slopes. She's the total extent of my family."

Ah-ha! So Terrific Taylor wasn't married. Blaze smiled. She should have been a detective.

"Is something amusing, Miss Holland?"

"Oh, no, I was just daydreaming. I'm afraid I'm dripping all over your car, Mr. Shay."

"Don't worry about it. Listen, as long as we're sharing something as intimate as sitting here in soggy clothes and, if we ever get out of this parking place, driving a dozen blocks up Sixth Avenue together, don't you think we should be on a first name basis, Blaze?"

"All right, Taylor."

"Let me turn on the heater. Are you uncomfortable? You really shouldn't have come out on a day like this."

"I'm fine. Please don't worry about me."

"Well, apparently someone should. Hang on, I'm going to make my move after this next car."

They merged into the traffic, only to be stopped moments later by the red light at the corner. "I'm intrigued with your Indian culture," Taylor said. "I've always enjoyed reading the history of the various tribes. In my opinion one of the finest authors on the subject is the Indian writer Benjamin Kiowa. Are you familiar with his work?"

"The light is green," Blaze said. Heavens, she couldn't tell him Ben Kiowa was her uncle! Taylor was liable to tell everyone he knew that the famous author's niece was an unwed mother without enough brains to get out of the rain. "Yes," she said instead, "I've read Ben Kiowa. He's also of Apache descent. Talented man."

"He's brilliant."

"Thank you."

"Pardon me?"

"I mean, thank you again for this ride. I haven't seen one taxi since I came out of the library."

"You must be a dedicated student to go study in this weather," Taylor said.

"Student?"

"You seem about university age."

"Hardly. I'm twenty-five."

"You don't look it."

She scowled. "Should I apologize?"

"Of course not. Most women prefer to appear younger than they are."

"I am *not* most women, Mr. Shay."

"That, Miss Holland, is a conclusion I have already reached."

"Now what's that supposed to mean?"

"You figure it out."

"I get the impression you don't approve of my marital status in regard to my . . . condition," Blaze said coolly.

"As I said, it's none of my business."

"You're right, it's not."

"Why didn't you marry the father of your baby?"

"What!"

"Oh, I realize we live in a liberated society, but have you thought of the child? Doesn't it deserve the benefit of two parents to raise it?"

"You've got a lot of nerve, you know that?" Blaze said angrily. "How dare you insinuate I can't properly raise a child alone?" What was she doing? she thought. She was starting to believe she was really pregnant! This was nuts. "Look, Taylor, let's just drop the subject, okay?"

"Whatever you say. I apologize, Blaze. I should have kept my mouth shut. It's just that . . . well, you look so young with your hair all wet and plastered down and your cheeks pink from the wind. I just hate to think of your being alone through all this."

"I assure you I can take care of myself."

"Whoever he is, he's a fool," Taylor said softly.

"Who is?"

"The man who let you get away. If you were mine . . ."

"But I'm not."

"No, not at the moment."

"Meaning?"

"That in about ten minutes I'll know exactly where you live and I just may decide to keep tabs on you."

"Whatever for?"

"For a while." He grinned, his handsome features softening with the smile.

"Don't strain yourself," she muttered crossly. "There's my building just ahead."

"Looks swanky."

"It's comfortable."

Taylor stopped the large car in front of the building and turned to Blaze, his long arm resting across the top of the seat. "Safe and sound," he said.

"Thank you again, I—"

"Blaze," he interrupted, picking up a strand of her wet hair and twisting it between his fingers. "I'm really very sorry if I said anything to offend you. Could I make it up to you? Have dinner with me tomorrow night."

"I . . ." Blaze was unable to tear her gaze from Taylor's mesmerizing gray eyes. What a mess. She would love to see him again, but how could she? He thought she was pregnant and she was not about to go on with the charade.

"Blaze?"

"No, Taylor, I'm sorry, that would be impossible."

"Why?"

"Because . . . just because. I must go in. Good-bye, Taylor." She started to open the door.

"Blaze, I will see you again," he said in a low voice, his thumb trailing lightly over her cheek.

Such a simple gesture, nothing fancy. Just a smooth thumb on the soft skin of her face, but it sent a shiver through Blaze that was totally disconcerting. In a breathless motion she lunged against the car door, remembering at the last moment to circle her arm under her lumpy bundle as she hurried into the building.

She would not turn around, she told herself firmly when she stopped in the lobby. She didn't care if Taylor Shay was still sitting at the curb. She was sure he was gone. I am now walking to the elevator, she muttered under her breath as she stood perfectly still. Then with a sigh of defeat she glanced over her shoulder. Taylor smiled broadly and waved, then pulled away from the curb and disappeared from view.

"Miss Holland?" a voice called.

"Oh, hi, Gus." She smiled at the security guard on duty.

"Um, are you . . . feeling all right?" he asked, eyeing her stomach.

"You mean this?" She nodded toward the bulge. "It's my . . . bowling ball. Yes, that's what it is. You can't get them wet, you know. Throws your game all off."

He nodded slowly. "I see. You went out in this weather to go bowling?"

"Certainly. I'm in training. Can't miss a practice. See ya, Gus."

"Good-bye, Miss Holland," he said, shaking his head.

Holding tight to her bundle, Blaze kicked her apartment door lightly when she reached it. "Good Lord," Murphy said when she opened the door. "You were mugged, raped, and got pregnant. I'll shoot the bum."

"Not funny," Blaze said, marching past her and depositing the sweater and the slightly rumpled papers on the sofa. "There. I just gave birth to the final chapter. Entirely painless delivery."

"I'll get started right away. There're pages for you to

proof and a tuna salad in the refrigerator. I whipped up some ginger cookies, too."

"Great, I'm starved."

"Don't forget you have that party at the Murdocks' tonight. I thought they might cancel because of the weather but they haven't phoned so I guess it's still on. Are you going with Brian?"

"No, he's in Los Angeles. I'll call Uncle Ben and see if he has a date. If not, I'll tag along with him. Otherwise, I'll go alone. God, I'm cold. I'm going to take a quick bath before I get to work."

"Have trouble getting a taxi?" Murphy asked as she scooped up the papers off the sofa.

"Actually, I rode home with a total stranger who was so handsome he brought tears to my eyes."

"Sure you did," Murphy said. "And I had an orgy with four guys while you were gone. I'll believe your story, if you'll believe mine."

Blaze laughed. "Sounds fair."

Ten minutes later Blaze had pinned her hair on top of her head and was up to her chin in a hot bubble bath. Absentmindedly she ran her fingertips over the cheek that Taylor Shay had so gently stroked. It was as though she could still feel the warmth of his touch, and the image of his handsome face and piercing gray eyes danced before her. Blaze was not unaccustomed to attention from members of the opposite sex. Her striking coloring and svelte figure brought admiring stares, and often unwelcome advances that she had learned to deal with deftly over the years. But Taylor Shay had unnerved her, sent shock waves through her body, and left her unable to breathe normally.

But why? Granted, he was extremely good-looking, she mused as she blew the bubbles across the top of the water. But he was rude. He had the gall to pass judgment on her for being pregnant and unmarried. And if he found her situation so socially unacceptable, then why the invitation to dinner? That certainly didn't make sense. Strange man, she decided, pulling the plug and stepping out onto the fluffy bathmat. Gorgeous, but strange. Forget it. She'd never see him again anyway. On to the tuna and ginger cookies.

The only sound in the large apartment for the next several hours was the steady beat of the typewriter as Murphy worked diligently on the last chapter while Blaze proofread the typed pages. The two women had been working together for four years, ever since Murphy had gone through a difficult and painful divorce and Blaze had sold her first book featuring the rugged western hero, Jake Stalker. Jake was half-Apache Indian, a hard-riding, honest cowpoke who righted wrongs and seduced most of the women who crossed his path. Blaze's uncle had recommended that she write under a pen name so that the public would think that the virile cowboy's creator was a man. Thus, Jeremiah Wade had been born, and no one except Ben, Murphy, and the publisher knew he was actually Blaze Holland.

The book Blaze and Murphy were working on was the tenth in the Jake Stalker series. The popularity of the tall cowboy had been phenomenal; most of the books were still in print.

Blaze, under the watchful eye of her Uncle Ben, had adjusted admirably to the sudden accumulation of wealth that her success had brought. Ben was a wealthy man in his own right from his books on Indian cultures and history. He had placed Blaze in the care of his own business manager, thus insuring her financial security for the years ahead. Blaze had also purchased her spacious Central Park South condominium partly as an investment, partly because her uncle lived three floors above.

Orphaned at six when her parents had been killed

in an automobile accident, Blaze had been raised by Ben. He had recognized her writing talent when she was quite young, and in spite of her moans and more than one temper tantrum, he had insisted she attend college, where she had taken journalism, English literature, and endless courses in American history. She had completed her first Jake Stalker novel the summer after her graduation from New York University. Since she had worked as Ben's research assistant and typist before her success, it was simple to pretend that she was still working for him and keep her true occupation a secret.

Murphy thrived on the erratic schedule and unpredictable timetables she kept while working for Blaze. They sometimes existed on coffee and doughnuts through a long night, and then on impulse Blaze would dash off to parts unknown to clear her head before settling down to work again. Murphy took it all in stride and loved the younger woman like a sister. Christened Annabella Murphy, she had taken back her maiden name after her divorce. Ben Kiowa had refused to call her Annabella. He referred to her as Murphy and the tag stuck.

Murphy was an excellent typist and produced nearly perfect final drafts of the books, correcting Blaze's spelling as she went. When thoroughly engrossed in constructing her plots, Blaze had a tendency to create her own spelling for words, but with practice Murphy had learned to decipher the strange combinations of letters and come up with the proper words.

Murphy admired Blaze's rare and unusual beauty and had become accustomed to the many men who constantly phoned and sought the younger woman's company, but she was not envious. Having once given her heart unquestioningly to the wrong man, Murphy was quite content with her life just as it was.

At five-feet-two she could shed twenty pounds and never miss it but, while always neat and well-groomed, her appearance was of little importance. She was Annabella Murphy and liked what and who she was, and she wouldn't trade places with anyone in the world.

"Hooray," Blaze shouted shortly after six, "it's done! We did it again, Murphy, *and* made the deadline."

"In spite of your trip to Sin City with Tilly," Murphy said with a laugh. "I'll have this copied tomorrow. Do you want me to take it over or do you need to see the editor?"

"I have no reason to go. I've already seen the cover for book nine. They've opened another button on Jake's shirt, the sexy devil."

"I love the part in that book where he makes love to the woman under the covered wagon. The whole time I was typing it I could picture some creepy bug biting him right on his tush."

"Jake Stalker does not allow such things to happen to him," Blaze said. "No bug west of the Mississippi would dare inflict such an indignity on that body."

"We should buy a covered wagon company, Blaze. Everyone is going to want one for the backyard after they read that scene. Think of the spark it could put back into floundering marriages."

The two women dissolved into laughter. Then Blaze gasped as she looked at her watch. "Where did the time go? I've got to call Uncle Ben about the party. You must be tired, Murphy. Sleep late tomorrow and just drop by long enough to file the research junk after you go to the publisher's."

"Okay. What do you plan to do? Are you going on a trip?"

"I don't know. I haven't fully recovered from Las Vegas yet. I'll think about it and let you know. I have some ideas flopping around in my head for the next book. Maybe I'll jump right in and get started. I'll see how I feel tomorrow."

"Sounds fine. I'll see you then. Have a good time at the party," Murphy called as she left the apartment.

Blaze sat on the edge of the sofa and dialed her uncle's number, smiling when she heard his gruff hello.

"And hello to you too, Uncle Ben. How are things upstairs?"

"Disastrous. That damn cleaning woman was here today and I can't find a thing. What's up?"

"The party tonight. Need a date?"

"I have one. Where's Boring Brian?"

"He's in Los Angeles and he's not boring."

"Yes, he is. All he can talk about is tax shelters and annuities. That, my dark-eyed Indian maiden, is boring."

"Well, you scared him to death. It's no wonder he gets all tongue-tied around you."

"Hey, just because I explained the special torture ceremony the Apaches favored for blond-haired men of thirty, there was no reason for him to freak out. I still say he's boring. I liked the football player better."

"You, maybe. I got a little tired of him flexing in front of every mirror we passed."

"Yeah, but he got us great seats to the Jets' games. Too bad you dumped him. Anyway, about tonight. Come along with Maggie and me."

"No, I wouldn't dream of intruding. In fact, this is actually better. I finished my book about ten minutes ago and I'm really pretty beat. I'll go around eight and leave early."

"Ah, so Jake Stalker is about to ride high in the saddle once again."

"Yep."

"Congratulations, Jeremiah Wade."

"Thank you, sir. I'll see you at the Murdocks'."

"Sure you won't change your mind and come with us?"

"No, but save me a dance."

"You're on. 'Bye."

Shortly after eight Blaze stepped from a taxi in front of a magnificent townhouse and walked up the wide steps leading to the double doors. The snowstorm had blown out its fury and the night was clear but extremely cold.

She was wearing a brown velvet floor length gown that hugged her slender hips and scooped to just above her breasts, and a matching coat. She had braided her hair and twisted it into a tight coil on the top of her head, securing it with several diamond-studded hairpins. She felt elegant, her mood buoyant with the book behind her, and excited by the prospect of the gala evening ahead. She handed her coat to the tuxedoed attendant and moved to the edge of the crowded room off to the left.

"Blaze, darling," Elaine Murdock said, swooping down out of nowhere. "How good to see you. It's been ages. You look stunning."

"Hello, Elaine." Blaze smiled. "Lovely party."

"Your uncle is already here and the women are drooling as usual. He gets better looking with age, I swear. You'd never know that man is in his fifties. He's with that cute little Maggie, the lucky girl. Come have a drink and then there's someone you just have to meet."

Blaze laughed. "Isn't there always? You're such a matchmaker, Elaine."

"Well, this one is different. He's so damnably independent there's no way any woman is going to get her claws into him permanently. Of course, why should he settle for just one? He can have his pick of the litter. Looks, build, brains, charm, he's got it all. But do come meet him, he's delicious to look at."

"How can I resist? He sounds better than one of your famous desserts."

"Blaze, he's the full-course dinner," Elaine whispered. "There he is over there. Lord, five women surrounding him. He's incredible."

"Maybe I should take a number for the wait like at the bakery," Blaze said under her breath as she followed Elaine through the crowd, still unable to get a glimpse of the man her friend was raving about.

Suddenly Blaze's heart started to race and a warm flush of embarrassment washed over her. She was now standing within a foot of Taylor Shay and his entourage of women, and Elaine was putting her arm through his to get his attention. She had to get out of here, Blaze thought wildly, but her legs refused to respond to her command.

"Blaze," Elaine gushed, "I'd like you to meet Professor, well actually, Dr. Taylor Shay. Taylor, this is Blaze Holland."

Taylor turned and the pleasant smile on his face was instantly replaced by a frown as his steel-gray gaze swept over Blaze's slim figure and came to rest on her flushed cheeks. "Miss Holland," he said, his voice cool. "You're looking . . . fit this evening."

"I—"

"Of course, I have read that the Indian people have great recuperative powers. I'm just surprised you could find a babysitter on such short notice."

"But—"

"What is he talking about, Blaze?" Elaine asked. "Taylor, you're not making any sense."

"Oh, but I am, Elaine," he said. "Blaze understands me perfectly."

"You know each other?" Elaine asked, her eyes wide.

"My yes, we go way back. In fact, if all you ladies will excuse us, Blaze and I really must catch up on old times."

"No!" Blaze managed to croak. "I mean, we mustn't be rude, Taylor."

"Don't be silly, my dear." He smiled but the warmth didn't reach his eyes. "Everyone will understand that we want to be alone to . . . discuss things."

"Oh, yes, of course." Elaine giggled. "Use Henry's den across the hall. Take your time, darlings. You'll be totally undisturbed in there."

"Thank you, Elaine," Taylor said. "You're very kind."

"I don't—" Blaze began, but Taylor gripped her elbow tightly and propelled her through the crowd, and across the hallway, and in to the den. He slammed the door behind them.

"Now," he said, his voice menacing as he folded his arms across his broad chest, "suppose you tell me just what kind of game you think you're playing, Miss Holland."

Two

The only light in the large, book-lined den was a soft glow from a lamp on the massive carved desk. The shadows danced across Taylor's face giving him, Blaze decided irrationally, the look of a threatening pirate. In his perfectly cut tuxedo and white-ruffled shirt his shoulders were amazingly wide, the broad expanse of his chest seeming rock hard under his folded arms.

"Well?" he asked, his eyes like chips of flint as he stared at her.

"Game?" she said weakly, backing up several steps.

"What would you call impersonating a pregnant woman to arouse my sympathies?"

"Now you just hold it," she said, her voice rising in anger. "You were the one who decided I had a condition, as you delicately put it. If you'll recall, I never said I was pregnant."

"What was I supposed to think? You'd eaten a big lunch? If that lump wasn't a baby, what was it?"

"Papers. Important papers I didn't want to get wet. Satisfied? I really don't know why I'm explaining this to you. It's none of your damn business."

"Don't swear."

"I'll swear, damn you, whenever I feel like it, Taylor Shay."

"Did you steal the papers from the library? Is that why you hid them under your coat?" He took a step toward her.

"Steal the—Are you crazy? Do I look like a thief?"

"Who knows? This morning you were an expectant mother. No telling what other occupations you have," he said, scowling.

"You're disgusting and rude. And you have a foul temper."

"You're no prize package yourself, Blaze Holland."

"I have had enough of your insults. Get out of my way and let me out of this room."

"No. What were the papers for?"

"Oh, brother," she said, shaking her head. "Okay, I'll tell you just to end this ridiculous scene. I went to the library to do some typing and forgot to take a box to put the papers in. When I saw the weather I wrapped up the work in my sweater and shoved it inside my coat. Get it?"

"What kind of typing?"

"Little black letters on white pieces of paper, genius."

"Cute, Blaze. Now tell me what you typed."

"What are you? An agent for the CIA? It was a manuscript for . . . my uncle. I'm his assistant. My uncle, by the way, is Benjamin Kiowa."

"Lord, now you're trying to pass yourself off as the niece of a famous author whom I told you I highly respect. Nice try, but it won't work."

"Ben Kiowa *is* my uncle," Blaze yelled. "Ask anyone at this party. In fact, you can march yourself out there and ask the man himself."

"Benjamin Kiowa is here?"

"Of course. We've been friends of the Murdocks for years."

"You're really Ben Kiowa's niece?" Taylor asked, his voice softening as he moved toward her.

"Don't you come near me," she said, backing up and then falling gracefully into a chair that caught her at the back of the knees.

"Been walking long?"

"Shut up, Mr. Shay. Or Professor. Or Doctor. Or whatever fancy title you use."

"The name is Taylor," he said quietly.

"Wonderful," she muttered.

"What did you do with all your hair?" he asked suddenly.

"What?"

"It's all wound on top of your head. I like it down around your face, or do you only wear it that way when you're pregnant?"

"That's it." She pushed herself out of the chair. "I've had it. This inquisition is over and I'm leaving."

"Oh? Just how do you plan to get past me to the door?"

"I'm not afraid of you, Taylor Shay."

"You should be. I'm bigger than you are."

"Is this where you pull your macho number?"

"Yep."

"I'll tell you what," she said thoughtfully. "Be a good boy and let me out of here and I'll introduce you to my uncle. Deal?"

"Nope."

"Damn you! What do you want from me?"

"Ah, now we're getting somewhere." He smiled. "What are you offering?"

"To you? Nothing, except maybe a punch in the chops. I don't know how to break this news flash to you, Mr. Shay, but I can't stand you."

He shrugged. "Minor detail. Now, it seems to me that you are in my debt. I, good Samaritan that I am, saved you from the ravages of the storm this morning. You owe me, Blaze Holland."

"Bill me."

"I will pick you up tomorrow night at eight for dinner."

"Like hell you will."

"I really wish you'd quit swearing. It's not ladylike."

"You, giant economy size clod that you are, do not bring out my finer qualities," she said haughtily.

"Eight tomorrow night. Wear your hair down."

"I have no intention of going anywhere with you."

"You have a choice here. We can stay in this room all night and let everyone's imagination run wild about what we're doing, or you can agree to have dinner with me and walk out of here right now."

"You're despicable."

"Great word. Well? What's your decision?"

"If I agree to go out with you, how do you know I'll even be home when you come to pick me up?"

"Blaze, Blaze," he said, shaking his head. "Don't you know me well enough by now to figure out I'll just camp on your doorstep until you show up? Your neighbors will love it."

"You wouldn't."

"Certainly I would."

"I hate you."

"Eight o'clock."

"No."

"Okay, get comfy. We're here for the duration." He sat down on the sofa.

"I can't believe this." She moaned. "It's like a bad movie."

"Tomorrow night."

"Oh, damn it, all right! But I hope you enjoy talking to yourself because I don't intend to speak to you the entire evening."

"Suit yourself," he said, getting to his feet and standing in front of her. "Shall we go join the others?"

"I'm going home, thank you. You've thoroughly ruined this party for me."

He grinned. "Need a ride?"

"Get . . . out . . . of . . . my . . . way," she growled.

Suddenly Taylor cupped her face in his large hands and, before she could move, kissed her lightly on the lips. In the next instant he pulled her tightly into his arms and crushed his mouth onto hers, parting her lips and finding her tongue in a long, searing embrace. Blaze's knees began to tremble and she found she couldn't move in Taylor's steel grip. Somewhere in the back of her mind she wondered where her hands were. Her eyes flew open in horror as she realized her fingers were tangled in Taylor's thick, dark hair, urging him closer.

"Until tomorrow night," he said huskily, close to her lips.

"I . . ."

"Good night, Blaze," he whispered, and then turned and strode from the room.

Shakily Blaze sank into the sofa, her fingertips pressed to her throbbing lips as she stared at the door Taylor had closed behind him. That did not just happen, she thought. She did not respond to that lunatic's kiss; she'd only imagined she had. Oh, who was she kidding? She had melted like soupy ice cream. And she didn't even like him! She couldn't stand him! He was arrogant and pushy and . . . despicable. He was right, that was a great word. God, the nerve of that man. He had literally kidnapped her, held her captive, and then blackmailed her into going to dinner with him. Creep. Rat. Nerd.

Restlessly Blaze began to pace the room. It wasn't her fault she'd kissed him back. He'd snuck up on her, caught her off guard, she decided firmly. He was a dirty player, that's all. But he had set off sparks in her she didn't even know existed. She probably would have started tearing the clothes off his gorgeous body in another five minutes. Lust. She had just experienced simple lust. Very interesting. Interesting! That was potent and dangerous stuff. She was used to being in control of these situations. Tomorrow night Taylor Shay wasn't going to lay a hand on her, that was for sure. He—

"Blaze?"

"What? Oh, hi, Uncle Ben."

"I knocked but you didn't hear me, I guess. Elaine said you were in here and then winked at me. I got the feeling you weren't alone and I wasn't sure if I should intrude."

"I'm quite alone, Uncle Ben."

"What's wrong, Blaze?" he asked, crossing the room to her. "You look upset."

"No, I'm fine. Uncle Ben, I really am quite tired and I think I'll go home. I'd rather not have to face that mob out there. Would you tell Elaine thank you for me?"

"Sure, honey, but this isn't like you," her uncle said, concern showing on his handsome face. Thick white hair covered his head and his six foot frame was lean and sinewy. His features were more pronounced than Blaze's, a slightly hooked nose adding character to the dramatic, high cheekbones. "Do you want me to come with you?"

"No, don't be silly. It's home and bed for me. Uncle Ben, do you think it's unladylike when I swear?"

"Where did that question come from all of a sudden?"

"Do you?"

"I don't know, I've never thought about it. You've got quite a temper, you know, and I suppose it has to come out somehow. Turning the air a little blue is better than throwing things. Why?"

"Just wondered. Good night," she said, kissing him on the cheek. "I'll get a taxi from here and just slip out. Have fun with Maggie."

"Okay, kiddo, get a solid night's sleep. You're acting kind of weird."

"I'll be good as new in the morning, I promise."

But she wasn't.

Blaze was crabby and irritable after tossing and turning through the night. The sight, the feel, the aroma, the very essence of Taylor Shay had haunted her through the slowly moving hours. At first she was furious with herself for allowing him to consume her mind totally, but after her third cup of coffee in the morning she decided it was entirely his fault and seethed with anger at the very thought of the man.

When Murphy arrived shortly after ten, Blaze was still clad in her football jersey. She greeted the older woman with the statement, "Men stink."

"Good morning, Sunshine," Murphy said. "I take it the party was splendid."

"I don't want to talk about it."

"Okay."

"Murphy, he's the most exasperating man I have ever met."

"Good-looking?"

"Gorgeous."

"Nice body?"

"Intimidatingly masculine."

Murphy laughed. "So far he sounds just awful. What's wrong with this man?"

Blaze scowled. "He . . . gets on my nerves."

"Meaning he's so darn sexy he rattles your chimes."

"He does not! Oh, hell, yes he does."

"Is that really a horrible situation?" Murphy asked, pouring herself a cup of coffee.

"Terrible."

"Chalk him off. Never see him again."

"I'm having dinner with him tonight," Blaze said gloomily. "By the way, I've given up swearing."

"Why?"

"Because it's not ladylike."

"Who says?"

"Mr. Arrogant."

"Blaze, you're not making sense," Murphy said. "This guy is beautiful, but you can't stand him. So naturally you're going out with him because look how chipper he's made you feel this morning. In addition, you're cleaning up your mouth for a man who does not approve of your longshoreman's language. Said person being the one you claim you'd like to toss out of a window. I think you'd better go back to bed."

"Maybe I'm having a nervous breakdown."

"Nope. You've just met someone who is pushing *your* buttons for a change. Sounds like he's in a different class from Boring Brian."

"You've been talking to Uncle Ben."

"Well, we did compare notes one day. Brian is dull. The football player wasn't too bad. This new one sounds super."

"Would you knock it off!" Blaze yelled. "Damn it, this isn't funny."

"I thought you gave up swearing."

"I'll start my new, virtuous life after lunch. Wait a minute. That's it!"

"Lunch?"

"No, don't you see? Taylor is putting this big rush on me because of Uncle Ben."

"Taylor who?"

"Taylor Shay. Haven't you been listening?"

"Right. Sorry. Carry on."

"Taylor thinks Uncle Ben is the greatest man who ever picked up a pen. I know he's dying to meet Benjamin Kiowa, and he figures he'll reach him through me. Brother, what a con job. I'm so smart, I can't believe it."

"Are you sure about this?"

"Certainly. I'm going to call Uncle Ben right now and warn him. Taylor may think he has an in just because we have a date tonight."

"I think you were right, Blaze. You *are* having a nervous breakdown."

"Uncle Ben?" Blaze said, after quickly dialing the number.

"The same. How are you this morning?"

"Great. Listen, there's this man named Taylor Shay who—"

"I'm having lunch with."

"You're what!"

"I'm looking forward to it," Ben said.

"You are!"

"My, yes, I've wanted to meet Dr. Shay for a long time. I respect his work."

"You do!"

"Blaze, for goodness sake, what is your problem? All you've done is scream two-word sentences in my ear since you called."

"Sorry. Uncle Ben, just who is Taylor Shay?"

"One of the finest journalism and history professors in the country. At thirty-six he's considered a boy wonder of sorts. He teaches, lectures, and writes outstanding papers on the importance of using accurate historical facts in fictional works. Fascinating."

"Oh," Blaze said weakly.

"Elaine introduced us last night after you left the

party. I was delighted when he agreed to have lunch with me."

"Did . . . my name happen to come up?"

"Can't say that it did. Why?"

"No reason. Well, have a nice day. 'Bye."

"Hold it, young lady. Why all the interest in Dr. Shay?"

"Just curious. Elaine was gushing about him and I just wondered who he was. Why is it you've never met him before?"

"He's on staff at UCLA. He's here on sabbatical for this semester at New York University. They're lucky to have him."

"He'll be leaving!" Blaze shrieked. Now why did she say that? she thought, shaking her head.

"In June, I suppose. This has been stimulating, but I must go. You're still acting flaky, Blaze. Take a nap or have a stiff drink."

"I just may do that."

"Good. 'Bye."

" 'Bye, Uncle Ben."

Blaze replaced the receiver slowly and then stretched out on the sofa, staring at the ceiling. Now what? she thought. Taylor didn't need her to get to Uncle Ben. They had a mutual admiration society going already. So what was the renowned doctor, professor, whatever, up to, holding her for ransom in dusty, dark dens?

"Did you die?" Murphy asked, peering over the top of the sofa.

"I'm thinking. My great analysis just got shot full of holes."

"Oh? Taylor Shay isn't using you to get to Ben?"

"Nope."

"Maybe it's just a simple case of the man wanting your body. I wonder if he owns a covered wagon."

"I'll ignore that remark."

"Your manuscript is at the publisher's, by the way."

"That's nice," Blaze answered absently.

"Man, this Taylor must be something. I've never seen you like this, Blaze. Before you go completely comatose, would you tell me if you want me to come in tomorrow?"

"Huh? Oh, no, don't bother. Take the day off."

"Great. I plan to walk nude down Madison Avenue."

"Fine."

"Taylor Shay, whoever you are," Murphy said with a laugh, "I'd like to shake your hand."

Blaze lay prone on the sofa for so long that she finally dozed off as the wakeful hours of the previous night finally caught up with her. Murphy filed the research material from the completed Jake Stalker novel, straightened up the workroom, set a batch of homemade soup on the stove to simmer, and carefully covered Blaze with a blanket. She smiled as she looked down at the sleeping woman. "Good luck tonight, Blaze. I think you've met your match," she whispered before quietly leaving the apartment.

Hours later Blaze stretched and opened her eyes, blinking several times before realizing where she was. Calling for Murphy, she walked through the entire apartment before realizing the other woman had left for the day. The aroma of soup filled the air and, not having eaten since the night before, Blaze consumed three large bowls and half a package of crackers.

It was after four and she knew Uncle Ben must have returned from his luncheon appointment with Taylor Shay. Curiosity nibbling at her, Blaze stared at the telephone, toying with the idea of casually asking her uncle what had transpired at the meeting. Hi there, she practiced silently, how was lunch? Is Taylor still the epitome of virility today? Did he mention that he's taking me out tonight under duress? "Oh, forget it," she said aloud. "I'm not calling Uncle Ben. Who cares what they talked about?"

She did, she admitted as she stood under the shower and shampooed her thick hair. She just hated that the two were all buddy-buddy after Taylor had been so rude to her.

Slipping on a soft blue robe, she dried her hair until it hung in a shiny cascade down her back. Staring at her reflection in the mirror, she lifted the heavy tresses and piled them on top of her head. Who was she kidding? she thought, letting it tumble back into place. She was going to wear it down. Because Taylor Shay had ordered her to? Of course not. It just happened to look prettier when it was freshly washed and hanging free. That was why. Wasn't it?

Wandering into the workroom, she sat down at the desk and pulled a fresh spiral notebook out of a drawer. Within minutes she was engrossed in the opening pages of the next Jake Stalker novel. An hour later she leaned back, propped her feet up on the desk, and began to read what she had completed. Suddenly she gasped, her feet hitting the floor as she stood up, and her eyes were wide as she stared at the sheet of paper. When Jake had gazed at the blushing young pioneer woman, he had done so with steely-gray eyes! Ever since his birth more than four years before, Jake Stalker had had dark, almost black eyes.

"Damn you, Taylor Shay," Blaze roared, and stalked into the bathroom for some aspirin.

Still angry, she locked the door to the workroom and tucked the key back into place under the potted plant in the hall. Both she and Murphy were extremely careful to complete the ritual whenever anyone was coming to the apartment. Precautions had to be taken to insure that no one inadvertently wandered into the workroom and discovered that Blaze Holland was actually Jeremiah Wade. Jake

Stalker was kept under lock and key and shielded from the prying eyes of guests.

For the next hour Blaze busied herself going through the kitchen cupboards writing up a large grocery order, which she then called in for delivery. Next she gathered up her laundry, including the football jersey, and placed it in the locked room in the hallway near the elevator for pickup. She could retrieve it in twenty-four hours, freshly washed and ironed. The minutes seemed to drag on, but at last it was time to prepare for the evening ahead and she opened her closet to survey her choices.

Let's see, she thought, resting a fingertip on her chin. What image did she want to invoke? Sexy? Sultry? Preppy? Ah, she had it. Wholesome. Innocent and pure as the driven snow.

Pulling a dress off the hanger, she slipped it over her head and zipped it up the back. Made of ivory-colored silk, the dress had a high-ruffled neckline that concealed half of her slender throat. The bodice had a multitude of delicate tucks, each encased in fine lace trim. Six tiny pearl buttons caught the long sleeves tightly at the wrists and a matching belt encircled her waist. The soft folds of the skirt fell to midcalf and matching satin high-heeled shoes finished the ensemble. A rosy shade of lipgloss was her only makeup. She dropped the tube into her clutch purse, then brushed her hair until it glowed.

Blaze nodded in approval at her reflection in the mirror. Taylor Shay was in for the surprise of his life. He pictured her as a hot-headed, foul-mouthed screamer, but tonight he was going to get sweetness and light. She would be wide-eyed and syrupy, and he would be caught off balance by her changed personality. The evening would be over before he had time to regroup and plan a new attack. He might have won the battle at Elaine's party, but tonight victory would be hers!

"I love it," she said merrily, dropping her purse and coat on the sofa as the intercom buzzed. "Hello," she sang out.

"A Dr. Shay to see you, Miss Holland."

"Oh, do send him right on up," she said, her voice cloyingly sweet.

Blaze used the few minutes it would take Taylor to ride up the twelve floors in the elevator to give her spotless living room a final inspection. Although it was large, she had decorated it so that it radiated a welcoming warmth. An Indian rug on one wall, a splash of color against the muted, earth-toned furnishings. Several woven baskets filled with orange, yellow, and brown dried flowers sat in one corner, and clay pots and bowls were nestled among the books on the floor-to-ceiling shelves that lined one entire wall. Throw pillows in vibrant orange dotted the beige sofa. It was simple but elegant and Blaze had received an endless stream of compliments on her decorating over the years. Now Taylor Shay would enter this room where she was in command, and she was ready. Oh, brother, was she ever ready to put Mr. Big Shot in his place.

The knock at the door startled her from her rambling thoughts and she slowly counted to thirty. Tonight *she* was running the show. "Good evening, Taylor," she said, smiling ever so sweetly as she opened the door.

"Hello, Blaze." He nodded, and stepped into the room, his coat draped over his arm.

"Would you care for a drink?"

"If you're having one."

"Scotch and water?"

"Fine. With ice."

"Please sit down, Taylor, I'll be right back," she purred, heading for the kitchen.

Wicked. He's wicked and evil, she fumed, as she prepared the drinks with shaking hands. Gray suit, white shirt, gray-striped tie. He knew damn well what that outfit did for his eyes and hair and tan. He was devastating and he knew it. The trick was not to let him know that she knew that he knew. "Lord, I'm confusing myself," she muttered, shaking her head.

"Here you are," she said, handing him the drink and sitting at the opposite end of the sofa.

"I like your apartment," he said.

"Thank you." Go on, she urged silently. Say how unique it is, how nicely the Indian motifs have been worked into the contemporary furnishings.

"It's pretty big for just one person though," he added.

"What?"

"This place. Don't you find yourself kind of rattling around in all this space?"

"I . . . No, not at all. I'm very comfortable here," she said sharply.

"Are you all set to go? I've made reservations for dinner."

"Of course," she said, getting up and reaching for her coat.

"Allow me." He held it for her. "I'm glad to see you took my advice about your hair. It's much more attractive like this."

"But . . ."

"Ready?" He smiled.

They rode down in the elevator, Taylor humming off-key while Blaze clenched her teeth together so hard her jaw ached. He was insufferable. Not one word about her lovely decorating and then to insinuate she had worn her hair down because he had said she should. The very idea! She happened to like it this way. So there, she thought, resisting the urge to stick her tongue out at him as they walked to the underground garage.

"I had lunch with your uncle today," Taylor said pleasantly, as he directed the large automobile through traffic.

"Oh?"

"Ben Kiowa is even more remarkable than I had ever imagined. You must be proud to be his niece."

"Yes, I am. He's more like a father really. He's raised me since I was a little girl. He claims I gave him every gray hair on his head," she finished with a smile, relaxing in spite of herself.

"I can well imagine. I bet you were one helluva rotten kid."

"Don't swear, Taylor. It's not gentlemanly."

Taylor threw his head back and laughed. "Touché," he said. "I deserved that one. You are really something, Blaze."

"It would probably be safer if you didn't tell me what that something is."

"On the contrary. You're a beautiful, warm, exciting, and unpredictable woman," he said softly.

Oh, no, she thought. He was not going to sweet talk her. "I take it you prefer your women predictable?" she said coolly.

"No, I don't. Not at all."

Now what was she supposed to say? Golly gee, you like little me just the way I am? Darn it, this wasn't going well, she thought, looking out the side window.

The restaurant was one of New York City's finest and Blaze and Taylor were led immediately to a cozy table. Blaze couldn't help but feel a twinge of pleasure at the surreptitious glances she and Taylor got as they crossed the room. She had to admit they were a striking couple. As soon as they were seated Taylor ordered an expensive wine, and, after the waiter left, asked Blaze if she was hungry.

"Always," she said.

"I suppose I could ask if you're still eating for two, but I won't."

"Not if you value your scalp," she warned, looking at him and trying to ignore how the candlelight danced across his handsome features.

"Actually, you were very lovely when you were pregnant."

"Taylor, hush. What if someone hears you?"

"They'll just think we're an old married couple with kids and that the next one is a twinkle in my eye."

"That's corny."

"Why? I think getting you pregnant would be very enjoyable."

"Would you stop it?" she hissed, looking quickly around her.

"By the way, who are you tonight? Snow White?"

"I like this dress," she said, smoothing the silky skirt.

"Like I said, you're unpredictable."

She glared at him. "Life with me is never dull, Taylor dear."

"Blaze," he said softly, reaching over and covering her hand with his, "I think life with you would be absolutely—"

"Taylor," a voice interrupted, "how are you, darling?"

Life with her would be absolutely what? What? Blaze thought, before tearing her gaze from Taylor's face and looking up at the tall blonde woman who stood by their table. Who in the hell was this? She frowned.

"Hello, Clare. Nice to see you," Taylor said.

Oh no, Blaze thought. Clare had a tan. This was the other half of the, "we had a great time in Aspen." Take a gander at the bustline! The blond skier made Blaze look like a boy!

"Clare, I'd like you to meet Blaze Holland. Blaze, Clare Scott."

"Hello," the women said in unison.

"Fully recovered from Aspen, Taylor?" Clare smiled warmly.

Blaze clenched her teeth.

"My muscles complained for days," he said, laughing, "but it was worth it. We'll have to go again soon."

The gall of the man. Planning his next little fling right in front of her, Blaze thought, taking a large gulp of water.

"Marvelous," Clare said. "Bill and the boys are already talking about it. We'll give you a call. Perhaps you can join us, Miss Holland."

"Pardon me?"

"Taylor is a marvelous skier. My sons learned so much from him. My husband Bill is still a novice but we did have such fun."

"Your husband?" Blaze asked weakly.

"It would be so much better to have another woman along. I was surrounded by all these brutes," Clare rattled on. "Do think about it, Miss Holland. If you don't ski we can always build a snowman."

"Thank you. I . . . You're very kind." Blaze's cheeks were warm with embarrassment.

"Well, I've got to go find Bill. He's gone for our coats. Good to see you, Taylor. Lovely to meet you, Miss Holland."

"Yes. Lovely. Good night, Mrs. Scott," Blaze mumbled.

Blaze folded her napkin into an overly neat square and then undid her work, placing the napkin carefully over her lap. Taylor's deep, throaty chuckle caused her to glance up at him quickly. He was leaning back in his chair, arms folded across his broad chest, a wide smile on his face. "Ready to apologize now?" he asked.

"What for?"

"Come on, Blaze. I saw the look on your face the minute you got a glimpse of Clare's tan. You had us pegged as love birds in the snow."

"I certainly did not."

"Okay." He shrugged. "Have it your way."

"You're right," she blurted out. "I'm sorry."

"I'm not. You were jealous and that's great."

"Jealous! Listen, I don't care if you take six women to Aspen and—"

"Would you like to taste the wine, sir?" the waiter interrupted.

Taylor grinned at Blaze, then tasted the wine and approved it.

"Would you care to order dinner now, sir?" the waiter asked as he poured the wine.

"Definitely," Taylor said. "My lady here gets very crabby if she isn't fed regularly."

"You're a dead man," she whispered to him.

Blaze refused to speak to Taylor during the entire meal. She simply pretended he wasn't there as she gave serious attention to her steak and lobster. A soft chuckle from across the table several times sent strange shivers down her spine, but she didn't raise her eyes from her plate. When the waiter reappeared she ordered coffee and pecan pie a la mode, which she devoured down to the last bite.

"Finished pouting?" Taylor asked, when she had drained the last drop of coffee from her cup.

"To what are you referring?" she asked, patting her lips with her napkin.

"Either you haven't eaten for three weeks or that was a splendid display of the proverbial cold shoulder," Taylor said, his shoulders shaking with suppressed laughter.

"If you recall, Dr. Shay, I did inform you I had no intention of speaking to you this evening. I just . . . forgot for a while."

"Oh, I see." He nodded. "Well, in that case, let's dance."

"I don't want to."

"Yes, you do," he said, getting up and taking her firmly by the hand. "And before you consider making a scene," he added, leaning over and speaking close to her lips, "do remember who you are. You wouldn't want to embarrass your uncle, now would you?"

"You're despicable."

"That was last night's word. Surely you can come up with something more original." He smiled confidently and pulled her to her feet.

Within moments she was held tightly in Taylor's arms, her small, firm breasts crushed against his hard chest as he guided her expertly across the floor. The aroma of his musky after-shave filled her senses and his hand seemed to brand her where it pressed against her back. Warning bells went off in her brain as she felt herself relax against his strong frame. She played a mental tug of war, fighting the desire that raged through her as he rested his sensuous lips on her forehead. One dance, she told herself firmly, and then she'd call a halt to this nonsense.

First the clatter of dishes disappeared and then the people. Soon the room had changed to a private cloud as she drifted along in Taylor's arms, lost in a delicious state of euphoria. The music played on slowly, seductively, and only for them as time slipped away in to oblivion.

"Blaze," Taylor said finally. "Let's get out of here."

"Of course," she murmured foggily.

She snuggled next to him in the car. His arm was wrapped around her and he kissed her many times on the top of the head as they drove to her building in silence. Still not speaking they rode up in the elevator and then entered her apartment. The dim light she had left burning spread a rosy glow over the living room.

With a soft moan Taylor pulled her into his arms and kissed her deeply, and Blaze trembled as she answered his demanding embrace with total abandonment. Sinking her hands into his thick hair she pulled him closer, meeting his tongue and molding her body to his. She slid her hands inside his jacket, feeling him tense as her fingertips traced the hard muscles of his back. His kiss deepened as he responded to her maddening touch.

She wanted him. Oh, God, how she wanted him. He had ignited a fire within her that only he could quell, and as his mouth continued to ravish hers she felt herself slipping away into a place beyond reason or caring. Nothing was important now except the need to have this man, this Taylor Shay, hold her, caress her, make love to her for eternity.

His hands traveled over her breasts and down to her slender hips. His touch strong yet gentle as he pulled her closer, his desire evident as their bodies met. Their ragged breathing was the only sound in the room and they were still standing next to the door they had come through only minutes before. Minutes? It seemed like hours to Blaze. Hours of ecstasy and she wanted more. Much, much more.

"Blaze," Taylor whispered huskily, taking her by the shoulders and moving her away from him.

"Taylor?" Her voice was hushed as she looked at him questioningly.

"I want you. You know I do," he said softly, "but . . . ."

"I—"

"No, listen. You are the most incredibly marvelous thing that has ever happened to me, but we're fragile,

Blaze. You're so mad at me half the time you can't see straight. If I make love to you tonight, I might lose you. You're liable to wake up in the morning ready to shoot me on sight."

"No, I—"

"Blaze, this isn't the time. The soft lights, the music, having you close to me all evening . . . You've driven me right out of my mind. I ache for you, but I'm not going to do a damn thing about it."

"Don't . . . swear, Taylor," she said, blinking back tears as his rejection seemed to burn a hole through her heart.

"Good night, my lovely Indian princess," he said, and after kissing her quickly, he left, shutting the door quietly behind him.

Blaze stood perfectly still, hardly breathing. She brushed the tears off her cheeks as she stared at the door. He had left her, walked away, leaving her burning with desire and yearning for the closeness of his lips and body. He had taken control of her senses, of her very being, and then tossed her aside. It didn't matter that what he had said made sense. The atmosphere of the dance floor had made her vulnerable and unable to think clearly, but she didn't care. She had wanted him and he had been noble and righteous and . . . wonderful. He should have made love to her so she could hate him and be done with it, she thought crazily. But now?

"Damn you, Taylor Shay," she yelled. "You confuse me. You muddle my brain. I despise you and if you keep this up I may . . . fall in love with you and I'll never forgive you if I do. Get out of my life! But . . . you sure as hell better call me tomorrow!"

Three

By noon the next day Blaze's nerves were on a raw edge. Taylor hadn't called and with a frown of self-disgust she stared at the phone, willing it to ring. She hadn't camped out by a telephone waiting for Mr. Wonderful to call since junior high and she wasn't going to do it one minute longer, she decided angrily.

She slipped on a bright red parka and a red wool hat and stomped out of the apartment. With her hair hanging in two thick braids, she looked more like a young girl about to join in a game of jump rope than the confused, frustrated woman she was.

Taylor Shay was an enigma, she concluded as she endured the long, slow ride down in the elevator. A mystery. He had managed through some intangible force to throw her off balance. He made her so angry she could hardly talk, yet he ignited such a burning desire within her that her need for him threatened to consume her. He was dangerous to her equilibrium and the safely structured, self-controlled existence she had created for herself. She didn't like it, not one little bit. She was fiercely independent and answered to no man. She chose whom she would spend her time with and for how long. Like Jake Stalker *she* made the conquests and then rode off into the sunset. But Taylor Shay was different. He called the shots, set up the game plan, and she didn't seem to have the power within her to pick up her ball and go home.

Hands shoved deep in her pockets, Blaze started east on Fifty-ninth Street, cut through Central Park and walked several blocks until she reached a small shop with a sign that read, "Tilly's Tearoom." A delicious aroma of cinnamon enveloped her as she pushed open the door, ringing the silver bell that hung overhead.

"Blaze!" A tiny, fragile-looking woman with a mass of silver curls on her small head and a warm smile on her wrinkled face greeted her instantly.

"Hi, Tilly," Blaze said. "How's my favorite Slot Machine Mama?"

"Just grand. I rented the biggest safety deposit box the bank had and put all my nickels away under lock and key. We *will* go again next year, won't we, dear?"

"Sure thing, but I'll need that long to rest up. You wore me out."

"Oh, pooh. I could have gone on for another three days. I was on a hot streak."

Blaze laughed and hugged the petite lady. Tilly had been a part of her life since she had been a small girl coming to the quaint tea shop with Uncle Ben for pastries and mugs of hot chocolate. As close as Blaze was to her uncle, Tilly had filled a need for her when she was suffering through the pains of adolescence. They had established a warm, loving relationship over the years. Blaze had wanted to tell Tilly of her success as a writer, but Ben had convinced her that no one other than the privileged few should know Jeremiah Wade's true identity.

"Come sit down, Blaze, and let me get you some tea. I just took cinnamon rolls out of the oven."

"Wonderful." Blaze smiled and settled down at one of the small tables covered by a lace cloth.

"Here we are," Tilly said moments later, placing the warm rolls in front of Blaze and sitting across from her. "Now, tell me what's wrong."

"I—"

"Don't say you're fine because I can see it in your eyes that you're unhappy. I know you so well, Blaze. Things aren't what they should be. Talk to your old Tilly."

"Oh my," Blaze said, unexpected tears springing to her eyes. "I can't fool you, can I, Tilly?"

"Not for a minute, dear. What is it?"

"I met this man and . . . I mean, he's so different from anyone I . . . But then again I really don't care . . . He . . . I . . . Damn," she muttered, brushing the tears off her cheeks. She was glad that there were no other customers at Tilly's at this early hour.

Tilly nodded. "I wondered when this was going to happen. It was only a matter of time."

"What was?"

"Until you met the real goods. A man's man, a strong hunk of stuff you couldn't tell what to do. I knew it would throw you for a loop."

"But . . ."

"Blaze, you've been parading men through this shop for me to meet for years. All good-looking, I'll grant you that, but they were putty in your hands. I thought the football player might be different but he was just as weak-kneed as the others. I don't think I'm going to survive Boring Brian," she added, rolling her eyes.

"Has Uncle Ben come by here lately?" Blaze snapped.

"Sure, he popped in the other day."

"Figures."

"The point is, Blaze, even though you haven't told me much, I get the feeling you're terribly frightened right now."

"Oh, Tilly, I am, and totally confused. Taylor isn't like the others. I get things all figured out and then he does just the opposite. I'm so jangled I don't know where to put myself. I think about him all the time, I get jealous when other women—Lord, are you believing this?"

"What I'm hearing is that Blaze Holland snapped her fingers and Taylor Whoever didn't jump. You're spoiled when it comes to men and you're used to having your own way."

"Tilly!"

"It's true. Since you were in high school young men have been falling at your feet. You're a beautiful woman and you're full of life. But that doesn't mean you're conceited, it's simply the way it's gone over the years. But now a real man has touched your heart and you want to run and hide."

"I'm afraid I'll . . ."

"Fall in love?"

"No! There's no chance of that! I won't fall in love with him. I don't want to."

"Why not, dear?"

"Because I have my life all mapped out. I like what I'm doing and . . . there's just no room for that . . . stuff."

Tilly frowned. "That's the dumbest thing you've ever said."

"I mean it! Love gums up the works. It takes up space and emotional energies that I'm not prepared to relinquish. I want to belong to myself. I won't give part of me away to someone, Tilly."

"Oh, Blaze, do you really think loving a man robs you of your soul? My child, you are so wrong. You lose nothing and gain everything. He becomes an extension of your person and you grow and blossom like a beautiful flower. Don't fight what you're feeling for this Taylor, Blaze. Give your heart a chance to find out if this is the real thing."

"And what happens if"—she sniffled—"I do fall in love with him and he doesn't feel the same about me?"

"Then you'll be hurt, but you'll survive and be a better woman for it. You will have experienced sex on a totally different plane and will never regret it. You'll have memories that you'll cherish for a lifetime. Then you'll pick up the pieces and start over."

"I wish I'd never met him."

"And you can hardly wait to see him again," Tilly said. "How old is this Taylor?"

"Thirty-six."

"Ah, perfect. Old enough to know what he wants and young enough to be a good lover."

"Tilly, you're awful." But Blaze smiled.

"No, just wiser than you. Get in touch with yourself and follow your heart. You'll know what's right."

"I think I'll become a nun."

"You can't, they don't allow swearing."

"I'm giving it up."

"That'll be the day. Eat your rolls and drink your tea. I've said all I can. The rest is up to you."

"I love you, Tilly."

"And I love you, Blaze, as though you were my own. I'll be here if you need me."

Blaze walked slowly back to her apartment, oblivious to the cold and the large wet snowflakes that were starting to fall. Tilly's words echoed through her mind and she shook her head often as she argued mentally with what her dear friend had said. Tilly had made falling in love sound like the greatest thing since peanut butter, but Blaze was unconvinced. Why would she want to leave herself open to such pain? Granted it might be wonderful at the onset to be swept off her feet in a rosy glow of bliss, but later, when it was over, what then? All that would remain would be tears and loneliness and long, cold nights. She had failed to tell Tilly the most important fact. Taylor Shay was leaving New York City in June. Heartbreak wasn't a maybe, it was guaranteed.

No, she decided firmly, this wasn't going to happen. She would end it now before it went any further. Taylor thought she was unpredictable and she would prove him right. She'd refuse to see him again. It was over. Done. Kaput. And she hated it already. Maybe she could get him to drop around once a day and kiss her so that—Lord, she was getting hysterical.

Blaze pulled open the door to her building and was halfway across the lobby before a deep voice said, "Blaze, there you are."

"Taylor!" she said, spinning around. "What are you—"

"I got a reprieve." He smiled and walked over to her. "The heat went out in the building I teach in, so they cancelled classes. Couldn't have all the little darlings turning blue." He tugged on one of her braids. "Little Red Riding Hood?"

She smiled. "Are you the Big Bad Wolf?" Her heart was racing as she took in his massive frame clad in a sheepskin jacket and dark corduroy jeans.

"In the flesh. Have you had lunch?"

"No, but—"

"Great. How about this for a plan? We'll eat and then go ice skating at Rockefeller Center."

"Skating?"

"Yeah, unless of course you'd rather go bowling. I understand from Gus that you're in training."

"Oh, no," she said, laughing. "That's what I told him the day . . ."

"You were pregnant?" He grinned.

"Seemed like a reasonable explanation at the time."

"One of these days your mouth is going to land you in jail. Come on, I'm starved."

"But, Taylor, I . . ."

"Don't you want to go?"

"I . . . Yes. Yes, of course I do." She tossed her head. "I'll skate circles around you, Taylor Shay."

"We'll see about that, Little Red Riding Hood." He kissed her quickly, then wrapped his arm tightly around her shoulders and led her out of the building.

"You know," he said, as they ate huge bowls of chili at a cozy café near Rockefeller Center, "I mentioned my teaching as though you'd understand what I was talking about. I don't think we've ever discussed what I do for a living."

"Uncle Ben told me. He admires you very much."

"I'm flattered. I really am."

"What made you zero in on this particular issue?" Blaze asked, reaching for her third slice of the thick French bread.

"I feel the use of accurate historical dates and facts is extremely important in fiction. Fiction writers have a tremendous responsibility and many of them take it far too lightly."

"I don't understand."

"Blaze, there are thousands and thousands of people across this nation who will never go to college or even finish high school for that matter. Their only link with the history of this country is through the novels they read. Unless the data is presented correctly they'll have a distorted picture of our heritage and the events that occurred that make us what we are today."

"I see. Makes sense."

"There's no excuse for the shoddy work that's being sold now. It has to be brought to the public's attention that they have the right to demand that respect be shown to our forefathers. The readers deserve a decent story, but more than that it should be set against a background of truth. Science fiction writers can portray the future any way they choose. Historical novelists shouldn't tamper with past events."

"Goodness, you certainly are adamant about this."

"Sorry, didn't mean to get on my soapbox. Ready to hit the ice?"

"Sure thing."

One thing was for certain, Blaze thought smugly as she laced up her skates on the edge of the rink, Jeremiah Wade wasn't guilty of the things Taylor decried. She and Murphy researched their little hearts out for those Jake Stalker books. Taylor would be proud of her.

The afternoon was splendid. Blaze had pushed aside her gloomy mood and haunted thoughts of the morning and thoroughly enjoyed herself. Taylor was an excellent skater and, when she questioned him about it he told her he had skated often as a child in northern Michigan. They stayed on the ice until the thickly falling snow made it impossible to glide smoothly, then went back to the café for huge mugs of hot chocolate dotted with fluffy mounds of whipped cream.

"Your cheeks and nose are all pink," Taylor said.

" 'Tis a bit nippy out there. Quite a change from California, I guess."

"Yes, quite a change." He was suddenly serious, staring into his drink.

"Taylor, what is it? You've gone all stony-faced on me."

"Blaze," he said, reaching over and taking her hand, "I hardly slept after I left you last night. I know what I did was right and the best thing to do, but . . . What I'm trying to say is, I'm not a superman. I wanted you and I still do. I have a feeling I've used up my entire life's supply of willpower on that one shot. You have knocked me off my feet, Indian princess, and you scare the hell out of me."

"I—"

"Look, we had better be up front with each other. I'm used to being Joe Cool, Mr. Slick. I've gone into affairs making it very clear that that's just what they were, affairs, nothing more, and when I wanted out, I left."

She frowned. "Nice guy."

"Honest guy."

"Well, pin a medal on yourself!"

"Don't get your temper all in an uproar, for God's sake. I'm trying to talk to you."

"So talk."

"Blaze." He sighed deeply and ran his hand through his hair. "The point of this baring of my soul is to tell you that it's different with you. I found myself standing out on the sidewalk in front of your building last night and I couldn't believe I had walked away from you. I trudged two blocks before I remembered I forgot my car."

She laughed. "You're kidding?"

"Shut up."

"Sorry."

"You're doing things to my head, lady, and I don't like it. No, that's not true, I do. But then again it's . . . upsetting. Am I making sense?"

"No."

"Thanks a bunch. Blaze, I've got this strange, niggling feeling—"

"Niggling?"

"Are you listening to me?"

"I just don't know what niggling means."

"Forget it. How about, itchy feeling?"

"Okay."

"Good. Now then, I have this strange itchy feeling that if I continue to see you there's a good chance . . . I mean we might . . . in time . . ."

"We'd go to bed together?"

"No, dope."

"We wouldn't?"

"Of course we would."

"Taylor, I think you lost me at niggling."

"That's it! I need some fresh air." He grabbed her hand and pulled her out of the café.

"Taylor, I don't think two dollars is worth going to prison for," Blaze said when they reached the sidewalk.

"What?"

"You forgot to pay for the drinks."

"Damn it to hell!" he roared and stormed back inside.

"Don't you ever again say one word about my swearing," she hollered when he returned. "What did the lady say in there? Was she ready to call the police?"

"No, I just told her my poor little pregnant wife suddenly got an afternoon dose of morning sickness and I had to rush you outside. She was very sympathetic."

"You didn't!"

"Besides that, I gave her a big tip. Come on, let's walk. We're supposed to be in the middle of a serious discussion."

"Which will go much more smoothly if you don't invent words as you go along."

"Niggling is in the dictionary. I just didn't use it

correctly. It means an unimportant detail and you are definitely not that."

"Oh."

"Blaze," he said, his voice serious as they moved slowly along the wet pavement, "what I was fumbling around about back there is that I'm . . . I'm afraid we're going to . . . get too involved and that's definitely not what I had in mind for my little stay here in New York."

"What!" she said, her eyes wide as she came to a complete stop. My God, it was happening to Taylor, too, she thought wildly. And he was just as concerned as she was. Do something, she silently urged him. Say we can't see each other again. He had to open his mouth and let the words pop right out because she didn't have the strength to do it.

"Blaze?"

"I . . . You caught me off guard. What do you plan to do about this?"

"I told myself last night I'd better end this thing right then before I got in over my head. So what happens when I unexpectedly get the afternoon off? I run like hell to get to you. I want to see you, be with you, and lord knows I want to make love to you. I should go back to California right now and eat oranges."

"You can't! I mean, you have obligations here, don't you?"

"Yes, I'm sewed up tight at the university for the semester."

"Thank God," she muttered.

"What?"

"Nothing."

"Blaze, I don't expect for one minute that you're struggling over our relationship the way I am and—"

"You're wrong! I'm . . ." Oh, now what had she done? she thought, her hands flying to her cheeks.

"Are you saying that—"

"Damn you, Taylor Shay," she shrieked. "What are you doing to me? I refuse to fall in love with you! I won't allow it to happen! I don't want this any more than you do. I have no time, no room in my life for . . . for . . . Why are you looking at me like that?" she whispered.

The warm, tender gaze in Taylor's eyes made her knees go weak. He slowly cupped her face in his large hands and kissed her, a soft, gentle kiss that immediately deepened into a searing embrace as he pulled her tightly into his arms. She clung to him, tears unexpectedly filling her eyes as she melted against him.

"Go for it man," a squeaky voice said.

Taylor looked up to see a freckle-faced teenager wearing earphones and grinning at them. Taylor smiled. "I intend to . . . man."

"Good for you," the youth commented. "Nice lookin' chick."

"Not bad," Taylor said, his eyes roaming lazily over Blaze from head to toe. "Little skinny, though."

"Well, I never!" Blaze stamped her foot then spun around and marched off down the sidewalk.

"Uh-oh," the boy said. "I'm getting out of here. She's mad as hell."

"She usually is," Taylor said over his shoulder as he sprinted after Blaze. "Hold it," he said, grabbing her arm when he caught up with her.

"Skinny? *Skinny!*" she yelled. "I suppose you'd prefer I had a bustline like Clare. One thing for sure, if she ever fell over she'd never hit her nose!"

Taylor whooped with laughter and then got mock serious immediately when he saw the fire in Blaze's eyes. "I deeply apologize for making any derogatory statements regarding the . . . attributes of your figure. Am I forgiven?" he asked, having difficulty controlling the smile that was creeping into the corners of his mouth.

"No."

"You can stay mad if you want to, but I might point out you're going in the opposite direction from the car."

"Oh." She turned around and headed the other way.

"Blaze," Taylor said quietly after they had walked for a block in silence, "we have a real problem."

"I know."

"Any suggestions?"

"We could . . . just forget we ever met."

"It's too late for that."

"You're right. But, Taylor, I really don't want a, um, relationship with you," she said, her voice shaking.

He nodded. "We agree on that much. But I'm not sure how we stop it."

"Maybe it won't happen."

"Maybe."

"Have you ever"—Blaze hesitated—"been in love, Taylor?"

"Old love 'em and leave 'em Shay? Nope. You?"

"No. It sounds about as appealing as going to the dentist."

"Some people really seem to thrive on it."

"The dentist?"

He groaned. "Get in the car," he said, opening the door for her. "Okay," he continued, once they were seated, "now what? How do we handle this? I don't want to stop seeing you. I can't. I won't. Maybe we should make a sort of . . . agreement."

"Such as?"

"That if either of us can't cope, that person bails out. No questions asked."

"Just disappears into thin air?"

"We're mature adults. The one leaving the scene

will calmly sit the other one down and explain, and that will be it."

"Sounds . . . reasonable, I guess."

"In the meantime, we don't date other people."

"Huh?"

"I won't share you, Blaze."

What about Boring Brian, uh, Brian? she thought. Poor guy was off in Los Angeles and here she sat shuffling him out of the deck.

"Well?" Taylor asked. "Do we have a deal?"

"Yes." She nodded slowly. "I agree to your terms. Do we shake hands on it?"

"Not quite." He pulled her into his arms and kissed her deeply, only to be interrupted by the smiling teenager who tapped on the window and gave Taylor a thumbs-up sign. Chuckling, Taylor released her, started the car, and pulled out into the heavy traffic.

Blaze stared out the side window, her mind whirling. This was crazy. Really, really dumb. She must have been in a state of shock to go along with this. But she had had no idea he was experiencing the same mental battles as she was. Actually, this was better. Now they knew where they stood. Everything was open and aboveboard. They didn't want to get involved with each other so they wouldn't. Simple as that. And, if someone got off the track, then they'd call it quits. Neat and tidy. Perfect. Then why was she so depressed? If he said one word she'd start crying.

"Blaze?"

That was one word.

"My God, you're crying! Don't do that, please don't. Oh, Blaze, don't cry. Why are you crying? Can't you stop? Here, take my handkerchief. What's wrong?"

"Nothing. Quit blabbering at me," she sniffled, wiping her nose.

"Tears blow me away. I never know what to do. We'll

go back to your place and talk, okay? *But please stop doing that!*"

"All right! Don't holler!"

Taylor kept glancing nervously at her until they had arrived at her apartment and he'd closed the door behind them. She had blubbered into his handkerchief the whole way home, unable to stop the flow of tears. Taylor had told a frowning Gus that they had just come from a terribly sad movie before he'd ushered the weeping woman into the elevator.

"I'm thirty-six years old," Taylor said, tossing his coat onto the sofa, "and I still fall apart when a woman cries. Ridiculous."

"I'm sorry," Blaze said softly, pulling off her parka and hat. "Would you like a drink?"

"I could use one but you sit and I'll get it. Where's the stuff?"

"Cupboard over the sink." She dropped onto the sofa and leaned her head back wearily.

"Here," he said moments later handing her a glass.

"Thanks."

"Blaze, what happened?" he asked, sitting down next to her. He stared at the amber liquid in his glass as he swirled it around.

"I don't know. I . . . Something went wrong when I met you and I'm so confused. I want to dig a hole, climb in, and never come out."

"I understand."

"Do you? One minute everything was wonderful and then boom! You walk into my life and I'm all in a dither. I'm very serious when I say I don't want to get involved. If this is even remotely similar to it, it's really the pits and I'll pass, thank you. We reached a sensible, logical agreement, but yet . . . it hurts. Don't ask me why it should because I have no idea."

He took a large gulp of his scotch. "Would you prefer not to see me anymore?"

"I'd rather be miserable with you than without you, Taylor."

"I'm glad you said that because I don't think I could stay away from you anyway. We'll stick to our plan. It'll work, you'll see. Getting too deeply involved is something that supposedly sneaks up on a person, but we just won't let that happen. We'll be very alert. What we have going here is a strong case of infatuation and physical attraction. We'll make sure it stays right there. We'll enjoy each other's company and later, part friends."

"Friends?"

"Yeah, friends," he growled, taking another deep gulp.

"I think you'd better go. I'm about to cry again."

"Oh no! Are you sure?"

"Positive."

"Would it be all right if I called you later?"

"Yes. Lovely."

"Okay. I'll let myself out. Keep the handkerchief. I guess you're going to need it." He frowned, kissed her on the forehead, and quietly left the apartment.

And she did need it. That handkerchief and two more until she finally stopped crying. Then she was angry. Furious. Seething at herself and at Taylor for the incredible situation they were in. They fought continually when together, but couldn't bear to be apart. Dumb! Neither wanted to mess things up by falling in love, yet both refused to give up the relationship, knowing that the risk was ever-present. Stupid! They had even agreed not to date anyone else, which would keep them in constant contact. Idiotic!

"Enough. I won't think about it anymore," she announced to the empty room and walked down the hall to her bedroom, pulling her braids loose as she went. Her hair was damp from the snow and wavy from the tight plaits, and she gave up trying to get a brush through the thick tresses, stepping into the shower instead and standing under the stinging onslaught of water. She stayed there for a half hour, allowing the steam to relieve the tension in her throbbing head and swollen eyes. After blow drying her hair she dressed in fleecy, bright pink jogging pants, a matching sweat-shirt, and socks. The soft material felt comforting against her tingling skin.

Wandering into the kitchen, she made a batch of macaroni and cheese from a box and consumed the entire amount, polishing off her meal with a quart of milk and the last of Murphy's ginger cookies. For the next hour she lost herself in the Old West and the adventures of Jake Stalker, then nodded with approval as she reviewed what she had written. She should have a good cry more often, she decided. This was excellent.

The ringing of the telephone brought her instantly to her feet and she rushed to answer it. "Hello," she said breathlessly.

"How do you do? This is Dr. Shay, currently of New York University, and I'm conducting a survey."

"Taylor?" She giggled.

"Please, madam, I'll have to ask that you refer to me as Dr. Shay. This is a professional call."

"Of course, Doctor. What can I do for you?" she asked seriously, a bright smile on her face.

"I am trying to determine how many beautiful twenty-five-year-old women of Indian descent are planning to watch the *Star Trek* film festival on television tonight."

"I see. Well, I'm afraid I wasn't aware it was being shown. However, since you've been so informative I would have to say I wouldn't miss it for the world."

"Excellent. Now, since you're the only participant who fills the requirements, it will be necessary for me to proceed to your home and join you in this endeavor."

"Am I a volunteer or will I be paid, Dr. Shay?"

"I'm sure we can work something out in that area. It will take many hours to view the festival since they're running every *Star Trek* episode ever made. Therefore, next question: Do you have any popcorn?"

"Popcorn?"

"You know, little kernels that you put in a pan and they go crazy?"

"Oh, those. Yes, I have some."

"Great. How about grape soda?"

"Popcorn and grape soda? Yuck!"

"Miss Holland, you are flunking this test! However, since I am such a kind soul, I'll furnish the grape soda. I'll be there in forty-five minutes. Good day."

"Good-bye, Dr. Shay. It's been a pleasure speaking with you."

"Yes, hasn't it, though? Until later, madam."

You are nuts, Taylor Shay, she thought as she hung up the receiver. *Star Trek!* She loved it. Her all-time favorite show. A history professor who liked science fiction? And he said *she* was unpredictable.

Blaze straightened the workroom and carefully locked the door, then washed the dinner dishes and dug out her jar of popcorn, a pan, cooking oil, and butter. Checking the refrigerator, she was relieved to see she had several bottles of cola; she was still skeptical about drinking grape soda with the salty, buttery treat.

The security guard announced Taylor's arrival over the intercom and she was smiling when she answered the door. "Hi," was all she managed to say as she drank in the sight of him in tight jeans and a black turtleneck sweater, his sheepskin jacket slung over his arm.

"Good Lord." He smiled, as he closed the door with

his foot, his gaze roaming over her pink outfit. "It's the Easter Bunny. From Little Red Riding Hood to a fuzzy rabbit all in one day. You're outdoing yourself."

"Oh, stop," she said, laughing. "I take it there's grape soda in that bag?"

"Enough for an army. We've got twenty-eight minutes before the show starts. Let's pop that corn," he said, walking into the kitchen and setting the bag and coat on the table. "But first, come here." He pulled her into his arms and kissed her thoroughly. "Feeling better?" he asked, studying her face as he finally released her.

"Much. Another one of those would probably do the trick."

"Glad to oblige," he said. His mouth covered hers, parting her lips, and she welcomed his warm, searching tongue. He buried his hands in her hair, moaning softly and Blaze returned the embrace with a rising, burning passion. Reluctantly he released her and gazed into her eyes. His own were smoldering with a readable message. "The popcorn," he said huskily. "We'd . . . better get to it."

"Right." She nodded, nearly hypnotized by his intense stare.

He suddenly turned toward the counter and roared, "Good grief, woman, do you call this a pan?"

"What's the matter with it?"

"Too small. We're going to make this up right. What else do you have?"

"Well, I've got a huge thing I make spaghetti in, but—"

"Haul it out here. I'll cook the corn, you melt the butter. This is going to be great," he said, rubbing his hands together.

Fifteen minutes later Blaze was laughing so hard she had to sit down at the table to catch her breath.

Fluffy bits of popcorn were strewn across the floor, counters, even the top of the refrigerator.

"Small tactical error there." Taylor frowned. "I thought it was done when I took off the lid. Got a broom?"

"We'll do it later. The show starts in a couple of minutes. You should have seen your face when that stuff came flying out of there," she gasped, dissolving into laughter again.

"Have you finished rolling on the floor? Here, you take the bowl and I'll get the drinks."

"I'm not sure I want grape soda with this."

"Try it. It's a superb combination. Trust me."

"Okay, but I have cola on reserve just in case."

"Have you no faith?" he yelled, following her into the living room.

A few minutes later Blaze shoved her bottle of grape soda into Taylor's hand and made a face. "Disgusting," she said. "That's awful. I'm getting some cola."

"Beauty, brains, but no taste!" He sighed heavily as she went back into the kitchen.

They sat on the floor with their backs against the sofa, the huge bowl of popcorn between them. Deeply engrossed in the adventures being shown on the screen, they hardly spoke for the next two hours except for whispered comments about the show. During the commercials they had a contest to see who could throw a kernel of corn into the air and catch it in his mouth. Neither was very proficient at the sport and the carpet was soon generously dotted with the white stuff. Blaze wailed when one hit her squarely in the eye and announced she didn't want to play anymore.

"Quitter," Taylor said, adding another soda bottle to the neat row of empties by the sofa.

"Are you building something?" Blaze asked.

"We did this once in college with beer cans. We had

them lined up all the way around the room. I was so smashed I didn't come to for three days."

"Lush! Where did you go to school?"

"Michigan State. So did Clare and Bill."

"Oh?"

"Clare and I grew up together. She's like a sister to me. She met Bill at college and they were married after graduation. I was best man at their wedding. She had one of those big, formal affairs and I had to wear a top hat and tails. You should have seen me, I looked like a six-foot-four penguin." He laughed, shaking his head at the memory.

"You're very fond of Clare and Bill, aren't you?"

"They're terrific. We all moved out to California, but then last year Bill got a promotion and they came here. They've got a house north of the city, in Westchester. It's been great to see them again."

"Clare said something about having boys."

"Three. Billy is twelve, Todd is eight, and"—he puffed out his chest—"my godson Taylor is a little more than a year old. They call him Ty."

"They took the baby skiing?"

"No, Clare left him with a friend and just the older boys went. She was sincere when she invited you to come along next time. I hope you will, it's really fun."

"I'd like that, and I apologize again for all the nasty remarks I've made about her."

"You're forgiven," he said, kissing her on the nose.

"Three boys. That's quite a family."

"Well, after the first two Clare said that was it, but she really did want a little girl. Bill did all this research. He read stuff like *How to Determine the Sex of Your Child*, and convinced her it was foolproof. When he came to see her at the hospital after she had Ty she threw a bedpan at him."

"She's not sorry she had Ty, is she?"

"Goodness, no, they adore that baby. He's super. Of course, he's named after me so what do you expect?"

"Does Clare work?"

"She has a Master's degree in Special Education, but she isn't using it now. She wants to stay home until the kids are older. It'll be a while because there's another one on the way."

"You're kidding."

"No." He laughed merrily. "Clare read all the material that Bill had collected and said he didn't follow the directions right. This time she was in charge and she's convinced it will be a girl. That's another reason she'd enjoy your company in Aspen. She really didn't do much skiing because she was afraid she'd take a fall."

"They're amazing people."

"True, but why all the interest?"

"I don't know," she said thoughtfully. "I guess I just realized that I don't know any families like that. Uncle Ben and I move in a different type of social circle. Clare and Bill sound so . . . wholesome, so special."

"They are. They could make a man believe in . . ."

"In what?"

"Hey, this is one of my favorite episodes. Watch the tube."

Two more hours passed in relative silence and the row of grape soda bottles kept growing.

"Oh," Blaze finally moaned, crawling up on the sofa, "my bottom is numb."

"Hold it," Taylor said, getting to his feet and pulling off his shoes. "You'll have to share. Move over." Blaze stood, her eyes widening as Taylor stretched out lengthwise on the sofa and propped his head on a stack of throw pillows. "Come here," he said, patting the cushion.

"There?"

"I won't bite you. It's big enough for both of us. You lie here and I can still see over your head."

"Well . . ."

"Hurry up, you're blocking the screen."

Blaze did as she was instructed, lying stiffly next to Taylor, her back to his front. She could feel his warmth and catch the lingering aroma of his musky aftershave.

"Relax," he whispered in her ear.

If he could handle this, so could she, she thought stubbornly, hoping he wouldn't hear the loud beating of her heart.

"Your hair smells like flowers," he said as his arm circled her waist.

"Taylor . . ."

"I won't say another word. You'd better pay attention to the show. I'll be giving you an exam on it later."

"Oh, brother."

Taylor seemed so casual about their being nestled together on the plush sofa that Blaze was soon totally engrossed in the exciting adventures of the "Starship Enterprise." Much later she felt her eyelids grow heavy and strove to stay awake, hating to miss any of the festival or the delicious sensations of lying close to Taylor's muscular body.

She would just shut her eyes for a minute, she thought sleepily. Just . . . for . . . a . . . minute . . .

Four

The next thing Blaze knew, someone was wiggling her big toe. Her eyes flew open and she stared at Murphy, who stood at the end of the sofa, an amused expression on her face.

"Good morning," Murphy whispered. "Having a slumber party?"

Blaze glanced quickly at Taylor. He was sleeping next to her, his face only inches from hers. One strong arm was draped possessively under her breasts, one leg flung across hers at the knees, trapping her in place.

"Not exactly," Blaze whispered back. "What time is it?"

"Nine."

"Lord," Blaze yelled, punching Taylor in the chest. "Wake up. You're late for work."

"What?" he said, sitting up so fast he flipped Blaze off the sofa and she landed on the floor with a thud.

"Ouch! Damn it, Taylor, that hurt!"

"Huh?"

"Come out of the ether," she said, reaching over and turning off the television. "You're going to get fired."

"No," he mumbled, flopping back onto the pillow. "It's Thursday, isn't it? I don't go in until noon. Have evening classes later. What ungodly hour is it?"

"Nine."

"Plenty of time." He pulled a pillow over his face.

"Don't you dare go back to sleep," Blaze said, poking him on the arm.

Groaning, Taylor sat up again and rested his head on his bent knees. "I'm so stiff. I'm never sharing a sofa with you again, Blaze Holland. You took more than your share of the room."

"Me? You left me about three inches."

"My, you two are charming in the morning," Murphy said. "You deserve each other. I'm Annabella Murphy, by the way," she said to Taylor, "but call me Murphy."

"Hi," he said, shaking her hand. "Taylor Shay, but call me crippled because I may never walk again." He pushed himself slowly to his feet and rubbed his back. "Are you an irate relative who's about to demand to know what's been going on here?"

"Goodness, no," Murphy said. "I'm an innocent bystander."

"Murphy does research with me . . . for Uncle Ben," Blaze said, getting up and stretching.

"Gus called on the intercom, Blaze," Murphy said, "but when you didn't answer I came up to see if you'd left a note. Looks like you guys could use a cup of coffee. I'll go make some."

Blaze yawned, then suddenly shut her mouth and looked at Taylor. The reality of where Murphy was headed hit them both at once. "Wait!" they yelled in unison.

"Good lord," Murphy shrieked from the other room.

"The kitchen is a disaster, Murphy," Blaze said weakly.

"What happened out there?" Murphy asked, coming back into the living room. "For that matter, what happened in *here?* No, don't tell me, I don't want to know. I'll just crunch my way through it and make the coffee."

"I'm going to take a shower," Blaze said as Murphy retraced her steps to the kitchen.

"Me too," Taylor said.

"What?"

"So don't use all the hot water." He stretched out on his stomach on the sofa and shut his eyes.

"You act as though you live here."

"I wouldn't dream of it," he muttered. "This place is a mess."

"Well, you'd better believe you're going to help clean it up," she said, and marched off down the hall.

Taylor was sleeping soundly once again when Blaze returned, dressed in jeans and a plaid cotton shirt. "Wake up, Professor," she said, walking her fingers up his back.

"Mmm, that feels good," he said, his voice muffled into the pillow.

"I put out clean towels and a new toothbrush for you in the bathroom. Come on, Taylor, get your body in motion."

"Oh, I'm dying," he groaned as he stumbled down the hall. "I think I have a grape soda hangover."

Blaze walked into the kitchen and stepped gingerly over the popcorn on the floor. "Coffee ready?" she asked. "I really need a cup."

"Just about," Murphy said. "So, that's Taylor Shay."

"Yep."

"You're right, he's gorgeous."

"I know." Blaze sat down at the table. "He didn't intend to spend the night. We just sort of fell asleep."

"You don't have to explain things to me. Gosh, he's a hunk. He's put together better than the football player and has brains to match. Quite a catch."

"He's not catched or caught or whatever it is," Blaze said crossly.

"Of course not. Here, have some brew. It might improve your mood."

"Tell me that's coffee I smell," Taylor said when he entered the kitchen a short time later holding a huge wad of tissues under his chin.

"What happened to you?" Blaze asked.

"I cut myself shaving."

"You've got a lot of nerve using my razor!"

"Don't you even care that I'm bleeding to death?"

"Would you stop it?" Murphy said. "You're giving me a headache. If you can't be pleasant don't speak to each other. Let me see your wound, Taylor. It can't be all that bad."

"It's nice to know someone around here has a heart." He scowled at Blaze as Murphy examined the cut.

"You'll live," she said briskly. "Sit down and have a cup of coffee."

"Thanks. *You* are very kind. Did Blaze tell you we watched the *Star Trek* film festival? Boy, it was great."

"So that's what brought on the destruction of this place," Murphy said, joining them at the table. "There's no way the cleaning lady is going to take this. She'll go on strike."

"We'll whip right through it, won't we, Blaze?" Taylor said, jiggling her arm to get her attention.

"Huh? I think I dozed off. I'm so tired."

"Work now, sleep later. Let's get to it," he said, draining his cup. "I'll hold the dustpan and you sweep."

"Let's just vacuum it up."

"Off the top of the refrigerator? Don't think so. Come on, Cinderella, there are chores to be done. We must atone for our sins."

Murphy propped her feet up on a footstool and thoroughly enjoyed the performance. Blaze and Taylor squabbled continually. She accused him of tipping the dustpan over on purpose after she had filled it and he retorted that her sweeping form was not exactly Olympic material.

"There," he finally said, "good as new. Not bad, huh, Murphy?"

"You two should hire yourselves out."

"Well, I'd better get going. I've got to go home and change into my professor clothes. I'm going to kiss Blaze good-bye, Murphy, but I'll tell her that just this once she'll have to keep her greedy hands off my body so you won't be embarrassed."

"That's very thoughtful of you, Taylor," Murphy said.

"I beg your pardon?" Blaze said.

"Shhh." Taylor put his arms around her and kissed her greedily. "I'll call you later," he said next to her lips, then picked up his jacket and headed for the door. "Nice to have met you, Murphy," he called before shutting the door behind him.

"Likewise I'm sure." Murphy smiled. "Blaze, you're in trouble."

"Why?"

"Through these portals never before has a man like Taylor Shay passed. Say, that was pretty good. Maybe I should become a writer myself. But seriously, what are you going to do about him?"

"Do?"

"Hey, he's all you could possibly want tied up in one package and he's obviously very fond of you. What happens if you fall in, you know, that four letter word you hate so much?"

"Love? Nothing to worry about, Murphy. Taylor and I have discussed it thoroughly and we just won't allow it to happen. Neither one of us wants that kind of involvement. And if one of us breaks the rules and loses control of his emotions, the game's over. Final whistle. Everyone goes home. So you see, everything is shipshape." Blaze walked jauntily into the kitchen for more coffee.

"Oh, yeah?" Murphy said softly. "I wonder who's kidding whom. Oh boy, I wouldn't miss this for the world."

The afternoon passed quickly as the two women worked on the new novel. Jake Stalker was to ride his trusty steed into the New Mexico Territory and while Blaze wrote, Murphy pulled out all the data they had gathered on the locale. Blaze consulted her encyclopedias often, double checking facts and dates and smiling to herself as she recalled Taylor's heated words about fiction authors doing this type of accurate research. The first chapter was half completed by the time Murphy left at five, and Blaze told her she would proof the rough draft, make corrections, and have it ready for final typing the next morning.

Having retrieved her clean laundry, Blaze took a long bubble bath and then sat curled up in the corner of the sofa in her football jersey. She had just completed the proofing when Taylor called.

"It's ten o'clock," he said, "and all is well. Isn't it?"

"Absolutely."

"How would you like to go to Clare and Bill's for dinner tomorrow night?"

"Am I invited?"

"Clare said to bring someone if I wanted to and I wanted to. You."

"Sounds lovely."

"I'll pick you up at seven."

"What should I wear?"

"Nothing."

"Taylor!"

"Well, if you insist then just something casual. I am now going to go put my bruised body to bed. You have bony elbows, do you know that? I'm all black and blue."

"Poor baby."

"I really think you should come over here and tuck me in."

"I don't know where you live."

"That's right. Wait until you see this place, Blaze, it's strange."

"What's wrong with it?"

"I'll let you be surprised. See, this professor from NYU and I exchanged positions for the semester. She's using my apartment in Los Angeles and I got this place."

"She?"

"Yeah, she's about sixty and looks like a wrestler. Nice lady but I wouldn't want her mad at me. This apartment was not at all what I expected having met her."

"Why?"

"You'll see what I mean. It's unique. Yes, that's a good way to describe it. Well, cute person, I'll see you tomorrow night."

"I'm looking forward to it."

"Blaze, I . . . um . . ."

"Yes?"

"Good night."

"Good night, Taylor."

Blaze fell asleep within minutes after climbing into

bed and had a strange dream about a cowboy who looked like Taylor commanding the Starship Enterprise.

Blaze and Murphy put in a solid eight hours of work the next day, both pleased with what they'd accomplished. After bidding Murphy good night Blaze headed toward the bathroom for a long leisurely soak, only to be stopped halfway down the hall by the ringing of the telephone. She rushed into her bedroom to answer it.

"Hello, niece of mine."

"Hi, Uncle Ben."

"Just checking in to see how you are and to invite you to dinner."

"I'm fine, but I'm afraid I already have a date."

"Oh no. Boring Brian is back."

"No. In fact, I haven't heard a word from him since he left. I think I've been brushed off."

"Thank God. So, then who's the lucky guy enjoying the pleasure of your company tonight?"

"It's . . . Taylor Shay."

"Shay! I'll be damned. How did you meet him?"

"That's a long, silly story."

"Is this the first time you've been out with him?"

"No, as a matter of fact we've been seeing quite a bit of each other."

"I'll be damned."

"Why do you keep saying that?"

"Because I'm delighted. Taylor is a fine man. Definitely the kind of person I'd like to see you associate with instead of—"

"I know, Boring Brian."

"Right. Well, I'll get off the phone and let you get ready. Have a lovely evening. Taylor Shay. I'll be damned."

"Good night, Uncle Ben."

"What? Oh, yes, good night, Blaze."

After her bath, Blaze stood in front of her open closet frowning. She wanted to look especially nice tonight. Clare and Bill were important to Taylor and she was determined to make a good impression. She couldn't remember when she had had dinner with a real family—a father, mother, and kids. What did people talk about when there were children around? She mustn't swear, that was for sure. But what do you say to little boys?

At last she selected a suede suit the color of doeskin. The pants were snug and perfectly cut, the tailored jacket nipped in at the waist, and she left it unbuttoned over a dark brown silk blouse. Her hair shone with a night darkness as it flowed down her back.

When Taylor arrived he kissed her even before he spoke. "Hello there," he said when he finally released her. "This is nice." He ran his hand over the soft material of her sleeve. "Pretty color, like a deer. That's it! Tonight you're Bambi."

"Tonight you're even more weird than usual," she said, deciding he looked superb in a burgundy-colored sweater and black slacks.

He smiled and cupped her face in his large hands, gently caressing her cheeks with his thumbs. Neither moved or spoke as they gazed searchingly into each other's eyes. The atmosphere seemed to hum with sensuality, the magnetism between them drawing them closer and closer until Taylor bent his head and placed a fluttering kiss on her lips. Blaze could sense his forced restraint and saw the fine line of perspiration on his brow. She shivered, a wave of desire sweeping through her, and took a small step backward, breaking the almost frightening spell that had shrouded them.

"You're right," he said, his voice sounding strangely hoarse. "We'd better go."

There was a tension between them, a newer, sharper awareness as they rode down in the elevator and walked to the car. Blaze kept her eyes trained on the toes of her leather boots. She was afraid to meet Taylor's gaze, knowing she would see smoldering desire radiating from those steel-gray eyes. Even greater was her fear that her message of need would be written boldly in her own dark eyes. Her heart was racing, beating against her breast as if it would burst. Her body seemed to be screaming at her to reach out and touch him, pull him close and feel the heat and maleness of his strong frame. She clasped her trembling hands tightly in her lap after she got into the car.

"Taylor?" she said softly, after he had slid behind the wheel.

"Yes?"

"I'm sorry that I don't like grape soda."

A wide grin spread slowly across his handsome face and he shook his head, leaning it for a moment on the top of the steering wheel. "Thanks," he said finally, squeezing her hand. "I needed that."

The crackling tension dissipated and was replaced by a comfortably soft and warm atmosphere. They chatted, laughing often as Taylor recounted stories of their days at Michigan State. He, Clare, and Bill all graduated the same year, and the description he gave of the party following commencement and their antics had Blaze laughing uproariously.

"You'd be surprised how fast you sober up when you spend a night in jail," Taylor said as he turned into the driveway on a tree-lined street.

"I'll take your word for it," she said. "My, what a pretty home."

The two story brick home was set back off the road and they walked up a cobblestone path to the door. Their knock was instantly answered by a smiling man whom Taylor introduced as Bill Scott. He was shorter than Taylor, wore glasses, and had thinning brown hair. The first signs of a bulge were visible over his belt. His voice was booming and the wide smile on his face almost boyish as he collected their coats and ushered them into the living room.

"A drink," he said, "and may I say, Blaze, that I'm delighted you're here."

"Thank you." She smiled, deciding immediately that she liked Bill Scott just fine.

"Taylor, you ugly jock," Bill roared as he poured their drinks, "you are really looking terrible. How many times have I said you should try to keep in shape? But no, you just let yourself go to pot. You know how it is with athletes, Blaze. After the glory it's all down hill."

"Now this is news," she said. "You didn't tell me you played sports, Taylor."

"No biggy," he said. "Where's Clare?"

"Fussing with the boys. She'll be down in a minute. Sit and drink," Bill said, handing them each a glass and waving them to the sofa. A leaping fire in the hearth warmed the room, which was decorated in an attractive and homey early American style.

"Been holding out on Blaze, huh?" Bill continued. "Old Taylor played football at Michigan State. Clare and I were his biggest fans. I still say you could have gone pro, Taylor." Bill reached over and whacked his friend on the knee.

Taylor grinned. "I'm not that much into pain. It's one thing to sit in the stands and scream your head off, it's definitely another when you're on the field getting massacred. I knew in a hurry it wasn't going to be my life's work. The football scholarship got me through school but after that, no thanks."

"Which meant we didn't get free tickets to pro games. Some friend."

"Good evening, Uncle Taylor," a boy said, coming into the room. He was tall, thin, and wore glasses. His unruly hair had been plastered down with water, but was already springing up on the crown of his head.

"Hey, Billy, how's it going?" Taylor said.

"Quite splendid, thank you, sir. How do you do, Miss Holland," he added, extending his hand. "I'm Bill Scott, Junior."

"Hello," she said, shaking his hand.

"My mother informed me of your name before your arrival. I hope you all enjoy your evening. If you'll excuse me, I must work on my studies."

"Of course." His father nodded. "Nice of you to drop by. Next time you're in town, give us a call."

Billy left the room and Taylor allowed the chuckle he had been holding in check to erupt. "Has he been in this condition long?" he asked Bill.

"Oh, a week or so. It's his super sophisticated, intellectual number. He's got a crush on a girl who gets straight A's and he's trying to impress her. He'll survive but I'm not sure I will. He informed us at breakfast that he wants to call us Bill and Clare, but Clare told him to take a hike."

"Oh my." Blaze laughed. "It must be difficult to keep on top of things when kids change so fast."

"Not really," Bill said. "We just ignore half of it. Hey, here's the middle son. Come on in, Todd, and say hello to Miss Holland."

"Hi!" said a smaller, rounder version of Billy. "Guess what, Uncle Taylor? I lost a bunch of my teeth." His toothless grin gave evidence to his statement.

"You sure did," Taylor said, peering into the child's mouth, "but you'll get new ones. Just don't take on any corn on the cob in the meantime."

"Okay. Gosh, Miss Holland, you're so pretty," Todd

said, his eyes wide. "Your hair looks just like a horse's tail."

Blaze smiled. "Thank you, I think."

"Blaze is part Indian," Taylor said. "That's why her hair is so lovely and silky."

"No kidding?" the boy said, crawling up to the sofa next to Blaze. "You're really an Indian?"

"Sure am. I'm part Apache. I'm named after my grandmother, who was called Blazing Flower."

"Wow! That's neato. Did she shoot bows and arrows?"

"I imagine she did when they hunted for their food."

"Did they live in tepees? Did you ever smoke a peace pipe? I saw on TV once where—"

"Todd, Blaze can answer all your questions another time," Bill said. "This is a grown-ups' night."

The little boy frowned. "Shucks. Will you come again, Blaze? Promise?"

"I'd like that, Todd."

"Great. 'Bye. Night, Uncle Taylor," he said, giving the man a big hug.

"See ya, sport," Taylor said, ruffling Todd's hair. The boy smiled toothlessly again and dashed from the room.

"He's darling," Blaze said.

"A motor mouth," Bill said. "Never shuts up. He's so curious about everything. Fun kid when he isn't wearing out your ear."

"Hello, everyone," Clare said from the doorway. "Sorry to be so long but slippery fish here didn't want to get out of the bathtub. It's so nice to see you again, Blaze, and how are you, Taylor sweet?"

Blaze couldn't take her eyes off the chubby baby in Clare's arms. He was dressed in fuzzy green pajamas with feet in them and his blond hair was a mass of curls. Large blue eyes stared back at her and she felt a strange twinge as Taylor got up and held out his arms to the child. "Come see your Uncle Taylor," he said, bringing the toddler back to the sofa and sitting down. "Blaze, this is Ty."

"Hello, Ty," she said, wiggling his fuzzy toe. "I'm Blaze."

"Bay," he said, not smiling.

"I don't think he likes me, Taylor."

"He's checking you out, aren't you, Ty? Want to see how smart he is? Ty, where's your nose?"

Dutifully a chubby little finger was planted firmly on the designated spot. Blaze watched in wonder as Taylor put Ty through his repertoire of finding ears, eyes, tummy and on and on. She saw the warm expression on Taylor's face, his pride and tenderness as he played with this human bundle that smelled of soap and baby powder. This was a side of Taylor Shay she hadn't seen. The large hands that once had tightly gripped a football now gently held the baby securely on his lap. The youngster smiled as his uncle praised his performance.

Suddenly Ty lurched forward, sprawling across Blaze's knees and she gasped in surprise. "Oh!" She turned him around so he was facing her.

"He's decided you're okay," Taylor said.

"Well, Ty, how's life?" she asked, melting as he gazed at her with his big blue eyes.

"Bay," he squealed, reaching out and grabbing a handful of her hair and promptly shoving it into his mouth.

"Enough Show and Tell," Clare said with a laugh. She retrieved her son, carefully unwinding his fingers from Blaze's hair.

"He's beautiful," Blaze said softly, reluctantly relinquishing her hold on the sweet package.

"Isn't he something?" Taylor said, close to her ear.

"I'll be right back," Clare sang out as she left the room with Ty waving vigorously over her shoulder.

"Oh, Bill, you have a wonderful family," Blaze said, her eyes shining as she looked at their host.

"I know," he said. "I thank God every day of my life that they're mine. And as soon as Clare gets this daughter in residence, we'll be complete."

"Guaranteed," Clare said, coming back into the room. "Do excuse my funny frock but I'm in that awful in between stage where I'm not ready for maternity clothes but I can't button my slacks."

"It's lovely," Blaze said, looking at the long calico print dress.

"It's a table cloth," Bill said. "Come again next week and we'll be eating off it."

"Speaking of food, I'll get it on the table. Blaze, want to splash the salad dressing over the greens?"

"Sure," Blaze said, following Clare into a large, spotless kitchen.

"I'm so glad you came tonight," Clare said, handing Blaze the salad dressing. "No, I'm going to say more than that. I'm delighted you're a part of Taylor's life. He speaks of you constantly when I call to check up on him and he sounds so . . . different."

"Different?"

"Happy, carefree. I don't know how to explain it really."

"I . . ."

"I don't mean to embarrass you, Blaze. I love Taylor like a brother and we've been through a lot together. Do you have any idea what it's like for a guy with his looks and build?"

"I don't understand, Clare."

"Women. Scads of them throwing themselves all over him. It's disgusting. Oh, I'm not saying he didn't enjoy it in college, because he ate it up. Lord, add the football hero bit and all he had to do was snap his fingers and they came running. As he got older, though, he came to see how shallow they were. All they wanted was to be seen on the arm of a handsome man for the evening and climb into his bed at the end of the night. He got cold, wary, and started building walls around his emotions. It broke my heart because Taylor has so much to offer. You saw him with the boys, especially Ty. The man should have a family."

"Oh now, Clare, wait a minute. I—"

"I know, I'm overstepping. It's just that Taylor says you're very special. Coming from him that means a great deal. Anyway, excuse my big mouth and just let me say again I'm glad you're here. Shall we feed our hungry men?"

Our men? Blaze thought, as she picked up the salad bowl and followed Clare into the dining room. Ours? As in, this one was Clare's and that one was hers? Meaning Taylor Shay was her man? For how long, Clare? Until June when he went back to the beach bunnies in California?

"Blaze?" Taylor said, coming up behind her.

"What? Oh, I'm sorry I was miles away."

"Let's eat, gang," Bill roared. "Blaze, I hope you're hungry because Clare is a terrific cook."

Taylor laughed. "She's *always* hungry."

The evening was wonderful. Blaze couldn't remember when she had had such a lovely time. Clare and Bill teased each other good-naturedly and she saw how often he gave her a warm smile or squeezed her hand. Taylor, despite Blaze's protests, gave a lengthy, dramatic rendition of how he had met her outside the library.

"Taylor Shay, I'm ashamed of you," Clare said. "Blaze is perfectly capable of raising that child alone. Heavens, you told the story so well I'm forgetting she really wasn't pregnant."

"He referred to it as my 'condition,' " Blaze said.

"Ugh." Clare frowned. "Where did I go wrong in your upbringing, Taylor?"

"It was sleeting and there were no taxis. A pregnant wife of mine would not have been out on a day like that," he said firmly.

"Oh, yeah?" Bill laughed. "Brother, have you got a lot to learn. Try saying, 'I will not allow you to do that,' and see how far you get."

"A busted nose for starters," Clare said cheerfully. "Let's go have coffee in front of the fire."

All too soon it was time to go and Blaze thanked Bill and Clare warmly, hoping the words sounded as sincere as she meant them. She hated to leave the snug, loving environment, the friendly people, and the three little boys sleeping soundly upstairs.

Oh my, she thought as she and Taylor drove back into the city, Christmas morning must have been so exciting there. Santa Claus still comes to that house and . . . "Rudolph," she said, not realizing she had spoken aloud.

"Who?" Taylor asked.

"I was just thinking what fun the Scotts must have had on Christmas morning."

"We did. It was great."

"You were there?"

"Yeah. They invited me to come from California, and it worked out because the semester at NYU started right after that. My mother flew in from Michigan too."

"Oh, tell me about it, Taylor. Every detail."

"The semester?"

"No! Christmas."

"Well, they woke me around five in the morning and . . ."

Blaze sat spellbound as Taylor reminisced about the recent holiday. She laughed with delight as he described how Ty was more intrigued with the bright paper and bows than the gifts, and how Uncle Taylor had spent a great deal of time poking his finger into the baby's mouth to see what Ty was chewing on. Taylor didn't finish the story until they were riding the elevator up to her apartment.

"The end," he said.

"Just like in the movies." Blaze sighed wistfully. "I've never known a Christmas like that. Oh, we had a little tree and Uncle Ben wrapped the presents so prettily, but it was always very quiet and we went out to dinner."

"Well, someday—Um, do you have your key?"

Inside the apartment Blaze slipped off her coat and tossed it over the arm of a chair. Turning, she was surprised to see that Taylor was still standing by the entry, his hand on the doorknob. "Did you have a good time tonight?" he asked.

"You know I did. They're super and it was a lovely evening."

"They liked you too. Isn't my Ty a neat little kid?"

"Yes, and you are a very nice uncle. Have you developed a lasting relationship with my doorknob?"

"You noticed."

"That you're still attached to it? Yes, it did catch my eye. Are you trying to tell me something?"

"As a matter of fact I am."

"What is it?"

"Come back over here."

"Taylor, this is silly," she said, but walked over to him. "Let go of the door."

"No."

"Why not?"

"Blaze, do you remember when I said I had used up my willpower with my gallant gesture of the other night?"

"Yes."

"It's true. If I let go of this door I'll take you in my

arms and I will not, I repeat, *not* let you go. I will make love to you, Blaze. Sweet, tender, beautiful love through the night and neither one of us will be sorry in the morning because we will have agreed it's what we both want. So, we're going to discuss it while I still have my hand on the doorknob and all I have to do is turn it, leave, and call you tomorrow."

"Isn't this rather . . . clinical? What are we going to do? Have a secret ballot?"

"Blaze, I know this seems crazy to you but it has to be this way. I don't want us to fall into bed because things got out of hand. I'm still so afraid you'll do something you'll regret and I'll lose you because of it. So this is how it has to be done. Very calm and cool. I want you, Blaze, but I have to know you want *me* and that you came to that conclusion without any unfair pressure on my part. In the meantime, I'm glued to the door."

Blaze studied him, frowning slightly. There was a lightness to his voice, a casual lilt that gave the impression his next subject on the agenda might be the weather. But as he took a deep, shuddering breath she saw his knuckles turn white under the force of his grip on the doorknob.

My God, she thought, he was doing this for her. He was letting her decide if the time was right for this next step, and it was taking every ounce of self-control he had to pull it off. Never in her life had a man treated her with such respect, given her such a feeling of dignity. Oh God, she did want him. She knew she would never regret giving herself to Taylor Shay. She would cherish those moments like precious gems and hold them in her heart forever.

"Taylor," she said, her voice hardly above a whisper, "take your hand off the door."

"Blaze, if I do . . ."

"I understand. I do want you, Taylor. I know you

need to hear me say it and I'm not ashamed to. I want you to make love to me. Now. Tonight. There won't be any tears or anger in the morning, I promise."

"You're sure?"

"I have never been more sure of anything in my life. You were right, you know. It would have been a disaster if it had happened that night we went dancing. But now it's different. We understand each other better, know a little bit more about each other, and share something special." She paused. "I don't mean to stand here giving a sermon, it's just that suddenly I'm frightened you won't come to me. I'm afraid if I stop talking you'll turn that handle and leave and then I . . . I'll be sad, Taylor. Incredibly, incredibly sad."

"Blaze, oh, Blaze." He slowly lifted his hand from the doorknob and caught her against his chest in a tight embrace. "It was so important to me that it was the right time. I've wanted you so desperately but I would have waited. Do you know that?"

"Yes, and that makes it perfect. Thank you, Taylor. You'll never know how much this has meant to me."

"Turn off the light, Blaze," he murmured into her ear. "We're going down the hall now and we won't be back for a long, long time."

Five

Fingers of winter moonlight crept through the shutters and streaked across the floor, casting a glow over the entire bedroom. Without speaking Blaze pulled back the blankets on the bed, then turned to Taylor. She took off her jacket and dropped it onto a chair then sat down and tugged off her boots. Next she slipped out of her silk blouse and slacks. She heard his sharp intake of breath as her lacy bra and matching bikini panties fell to the floor and she stood before him in naked splendor.

"You're beautiful, Blaze," he said huskily, standing close to her but not touching her. "Very beautiful. I want this to be so good but . . . I don't think I have one ounce of control left. I might rush you and—"

"Hush," she said, placing her fingertips on his lips. "I know that. We have all night, Taylor, to discover everything we want to know about each other. I saw what it took for you to stand by that door, fighting your own needs so it would be right for me. Come to me now, for yourself, and later we'll be really together."

"My God," he moaned softly, pulling her into his arms and kissing her deeply.

When he released her she lay back on the bed and watched as he shed his clothing, seeing how his hands trembled slightly as he pulled the sweater over his head. Her heart quickened at the sight of his muscled chest covered by a mass of curly black hair, his shoulders wide and strong. The sight of his narrow hips as he neared the bed sent a surge of heat through her body, and she shut her eyes for a moment as a wave of dizziness swept over her. Then he was lying next to her, his massive frame stretched out, every inch of him announcing his masculinity. Her senses were overwhelmed by his closeness, the heat emanating from his body, the heady smell of the brandy they had drunk after dinner, the tangy odor of male perspiration.

Slowly he ran his hand across her stomach, then up to her breasts, and she felt the tremor in his fingers. His hand cupped her breast, lovingly learning their shape, while his fingers teased the erect nipples until Blaze moaned with desire.

Taylor shifted, bringing his mouth to hers and kissed her, first sweetly and tenderly, then with a growing passion that Blaze matched. His hand left her breasts and slipped down her side, sliding across her stomach, palming her lean hip, massaging her thigh. Blaze's own hands were eagerly exploring his body, the solid chest, his long, smooth back. Taylor lifted his head and stared into her eyes as his hand slid between her thighs to her heated center. Blaze gasped and arched her hips, her arms tightening about him.

"Oh, Blaze," he murmured. "I can't wait any—"

"Now, Taylor," she whispered. "Make love to me now."

He moved over her and she welcomed his weight as he smoothly entered her. She wrapped her arms around him, urging him closer, relishing the feel of his muscles straining under her touch. Passion exploded deep within her and she arched her back to meet his driving force, catching his rhythm, staying with him. This was to have been for him, she thought as she slipped away to a place beyond reason, but they had gone together. She had wanted only to give, but now she was taking as well. But that was fine, wonderful, fanta—

"Oh God, Taylor," she gasped as a kaleidoscope of colors burst before her eyes. She held him tightly, afraid that if she let go she would float away and never return.

"Blaze," he murmured into her hair, "my Blaze."

Gently Taylor pulled her to his side. His body was glistening with perspiration and she trailed her fingertips through the rough hair on his chest, over the moist, taut skin as he stroked her breasts. Each embarked on a tantalizing journey of exploration of the other, touching, caressing, kissing. Time had no meaning as the discoveries were made, savored, memorized for eternity. Their breathing quickened and their hands and lips moved more possessively, staking claim to what they found, desired, and would have as their own.

"I'll never get enough of you, Blaze," he said, as he pulled her on top of him.

"Always want me, Taylor," she said, lowering her mouth to his.

They came together slowly, each holding back, wanting the moment to last forever. Then the flame burst within them and consumed them in body and mind. They soared to heights never before achieved, lingered there, partaking of the ecstasy, then slowly drifted back to now.

Blaze blinked several times as the room came into focus. Everything was the same. The bed, the dresser, the carpet, were all just as they had been. But she felt she had never seen any of it before. She was changed, different. Where was this place she had gone to with Taylor? She had climbed beyond reality and reason to a new world. There was only one man capable of taking her there and bringing her safely back. Her body had been awakened from lifelong slumber, been given a fresh meaning. But who was she now that Taylor Shay had opened doors she hadn't known existed? Could she ever again claim herself as her own, or did he possess her, controlling her reasoning and purpose? Suddenly she shivered, not from a chill but from fear. Was she lost? Had she passed into his hands the very essence of her being?

"Blaze?" he said softly. "Is anything wrong?"

"I'm frightened, Taylor," she said, reaching out and gripping his arm.

"Of what?"

"I've never known such . . . I can't explain it. It's as though I've been away, gone somewhere with you that I haven't seen before and now I'm back. It's almost like being outside of myself watching the changes. My body . . . acted on its own, responded like it belonged to you, not me."

"Blaze, you gave yourself totally. You kept nothing from me. That's not a surrender of your identity, it's a precious gift, and I'll treat it as such. Don't be afraid of what happened. You've experienced what some women never do. We were together, Blaze, as one, and it was wonderful. You've had sex before, but tonight we made love. There's a big difference. Do you understand?"

"Yes. Yes, I do. It's as though there's never been anyone but you. Oh, Taylor, I feel so alive, so real."

"Are you still frightened?"

"No, not anymore." She laughed suddenly. "I may, however, turn into a nymphomaniac."

"Sounds good to me," he chuckled, nuzzling her neck.

"Oh, I'm so sleepy. I feel like a contented old cow."

"Then close your big dark eyes." He pulled her close. "Damn."

"What's the matter?"

"I've got a class to teach in a few hours. Have you got an alarm clock?"

"Yuck, now you're getting practical." She reached over to the nightstand. "What time do you want this thing to scream its head off?"

"Six."

"Damn is right."

"I'll probably stand up in front of those students with a silly grin on my face. They'll think, 'Ah-ha, stuffy old Professor Shay has the look of a man who has been thoroughly made love to.' "

"Are you really stuffy?"

"Sure. I wear three-piece suits and frown a lot. I'm waiting to get gray hair over my temples so I'll look distinguished."

"I bet the girls all swoon."

"I've got a scrapbook of all the racy notes they've shoved under my office door."

"Seriously?"

"Nope. Go to sleep, pretty lady," he said, kissing her quickly.

"Okay, pretty man." She snuggled next to him, sharing his pillow.

They slept deeply and dreamlessly, entwined in each other's arms. Blaze stirred once and tried to move but Taylor's arm, resting beneath her breasts, tightened slightly so she couldn't leave him. She settled back against his warm body, her response to his touch natural, automatic.

Taylor groaned when the alarm shattered the still air. Without opening her eyes Blaze fumbled in the dark and shut it off. "Rude," she muttered, flopping back onto the pillow. "Are you awake, Taylor? Taylor?"

"No."

"Wake up."

"No."

"You were the one who wanted the alarm set. You are planning to teach today, aren't you?"

"No."

"Would you quit saying 'no.' "

"No."

"Okay, I'm warning you. I'm going back to sleep and if you're late it's just your tough luck."

"Oh, yeah?" He rolled over on top of her.

"You were wide awake the whole time, you idiot."

"You look so pretty with your hair all spread out over the pillow. You are, Blaze Holland, a beautiful woman."

"This hair? Todd says it looks like a horse's tail."

"Coming from an eight-year-old, that's a compliment. Bigger boys, like me for instance, are more inclined to go for the whole package." He kissed her eyes, her nose, then moved down her slender throat with light, nibbling kisses that sent familiar and welcomed signals through her body.

"You . . . have a . . . class, remember?" she asked breathlessly, trailing her hands over his back and beyond.

"That's why I set the alarm for six. Didn't want to have to . . . rush."

"Good thinking, professor," she said, just before he covered her mouth in a fierce, passionate kiss.

Much later Blaze lay staring at the ceiling, a smile on her face as she listened to Taylor singing terribly off-key in the shower. Lazily she pushed herself off the bed and donned a pair of bikini panties. She was just dropping her football jersey over her head when Taylor emerged from the bathroom, clad only in a towel draped low on his hips.

"Good Lord," he shouted, "I just spent the night making love to one of the New York Jets!"

"This is my nightie. I'm going back to sleep after I fix you some breakfast and send you out to earn a living."

"Hey," he said, fingering the material of the jersey, "I played football long enough to know this is the real thing. It didn't come from a department store."

"Oh, really?"

"But I won't ask any questions. None of my business, you see."

"How do you want your eggs?"

"Cooked."

"Cute."

"Whatever, I don't care. An egg is an egg. Surprise me."

"I think I'll stand here and watch you get dressed."

"That's kind of kinky, but suit yourself. I want you to know I cut myself with your lousy razor again."

"Then quit using it!"

"Go fry an egg."

"Okay," she said merrily, and headed for the kitchen.

Fifteen minutes later Blaze sat across the table from Taylor, her chin propped in her hand as she watched him with wonder. He had very slowly and carefully spread butter in smooth, even strokes over a piece of toast and then set the toast on the side of his plate. Picking up another piece, he had covered that one with jelly, making sure the edges were even as he held it to eye level to view his work.

"Weird," she observed. "Definitely weird."

"Well, my dear, it's really quite simple. I like butter. I like jelly. I do not, however, care for butter and jelly together."

"Interesting."

"You are the only woman, besides my mother of course, who knows that terrific bit of information about me."

"Oh, come on, Taylor, give me a break. Are you trying to infer that I'm the first member of the opposite sex you've ever shared a morning after with?"

"I didn't say that. The message is you're the first to care enough to notice how I eat my toast."

"Oh," she said, realizing he was perfectly serious. "I see."

"Do you?" he asked softly, running his thumb lightly over her lips. "Tell me a secret, Blaze. Share something with me no one else knows."

"Why?"

"Because now you know about my toast and this is a fifty-fifty relationship. You owe me one."

"You really mean it, don't you?"

"Yes."

"Oh my," she said, taking a deep breath. "There's only one thing that's really mine, but I guess . . . I could tell you."

"Go ahead."

"Butterflies."

"And?"

"It's dumb, but here goes. I sneak over to Central Park and watch the butterflies. They're so delicate and beautiful and free. But they've worked so hard to be what they are. They inched their way along the ground as caterpillars and spent time in captivity in a cocoon. Then, Taylor, it's their turn to fly in the sunshine and dance through the flowers. They make me, I don't know, feel that if you keep on trying things will turn out all right. I . . . this is embarrassing."

"Thank you, Blaze," he said. "I mean that very sincerely."

"Quit looking at me like that or you may not get to your first class after all."

"Don't tempt me," he chuckled, poking a forkful of eggs into his mouth.

Suddenly the intercom buzzed and Blaze looked up in surprise. "Who in the . . . Oh no, I forgot! Murphy said she was coming early because she has a dentist appointment later." She hurried to the speaker. "Yes?"

"Miss Murphy is here, Miss Holland."

"Okay. Have her come on up, please." She turned back to Taylor. "Just eat your eggs and look innocent."

"It's not as if she's your mother or something, Blaze."

"True. I'll hand her a cup of coffee as she walks in. Maybe she won't notice you're sitting there."

"Murphy is a together lady, she'll understand," Taylor said, buttering another slice of toast.

"We'll know in a minute," Blaze said, going to answer the knock at the door.

"Hi, Blaze," Murphy said. "Any coffee?" She walked into the kitchen. "Oh, good morning, Taylor. Did you manage to shave this morning without cutting yourself?"

"Hell, no. Blaze has a really crummy razor."

"You ought to start toting your own. Scoot over, I'm not working until I've drunk this cup down to the last drop."

Blaze and Taylor exchanged delighted smiles over Murphy's reaction to what could have been an awkward situation, and the three chatted amicably while

Taylor finished his breakfast. "Well," he said, pushing his plate away, "thank you. That was tasty but I've got to hustle."

"I'll walk you to the door," Blaze said, getting up.

In the living room Taylor shrugged into his coat and turned to her, tracing the numbers on the football jersey with his long finger. "I know I shouldn't say this but . . ."

"Get rid of the jersey."

"Yes."

"You've got it. I'm not sentimentally attached to it, it's just comfortable."

"I'll buy you something else. I'm just not really up for sharing my bed with an *authentic* New York Jet, if you get the drift."

"I do. No problem. Are you really going to buy me a new nightie?"

"Sure, but not one of those frilly, peekaboo things, due to the fact you wouldn't find me lurking around a lingerie department. It'll be neat though, you'll see."

She laughed. "This ought to be good."

"Listen, how about coming over to my place tonight? We'll pick up some Chinese take-out food."

"Sounds like fun. I'm anxious to see this mysterious abode of yours."

"Don't blame me if you have nightmares. Man, I'm late. I'll pick you up around seven. Kiss me, woman, I'm in a hurry."

And she did kiss him—a long, lingering, deeply passionate kiss that neither wished to end. Finally Taylor took her firmly by the arms and detached her from his body. "Hold that thought," he said, his voice husky. "Don't forget, ditch the shirt. 'Bye, Murphy," he called as he left the apartment.

"Ta-ta," Murphy hollered after him.

Blaze wandered slowly back into the kitchen and absently poured herself another cup of coffee, then sat down opposite Murphy at the table. "I'll have this jersey laundered and then you can have it if you want it, Murphy," she said.

"You're giving up your football jersey for Taylor Shay?"

"Well, I mean, it's not that big a deal."

"I do believe I had instructions to bury you in it when you die."

"That's only because I'm used to it. I hate sleeping in those satin things that stick to my body. My attachment to it has nothing to do with the muscle-brain that gave it to me."

"But Taylor doesn't like it, right?"

"He played football and knows it's a regulation shirt. He—"

"Doesn't want the ghost of a Jet floating around the bedroom with you two?"

"Murphy! I never said Taylor was in my bedroom!"

"Of course not. He just dropped in for breakfast and a shave. Do I look stupid or something? I don't know what you're getting all in a huff about. You and Taylor are healthy, attractive people. It's only natural you'd want to enjoy the physical side of your relationship. Besides, how important can it be?"

"What?"

"After all, you have an understanding. There's no love involved here. You'll have a good time for a while and then mosey on down the trail like old Stalker. That's how it is, right?"

"Um, sure. That's absolutely . . . right," Blaze said, staring into her cup.

"Well, I'm going to get to work," Murphy said and quickly left the room before Blaze could see the mischief dancing in her eyes.

Just before seven that evening Blaze glanced in the mirror and straightened the collar on her cream-colored silk blouse, then smoothed her green velvet pants. It was perhaps a little dressy for take-out Chinese food, but she felt pretty and feminine and special and had dressed accordingly. She knew her lovemaking with Taylor had sharpened her awareness of herself. He had unlocked a part of her mind and body, bringing forth a new dimension that was exciting and invigorating.

Taylor's name had not come up again during their long day of work. Blaze had exercised the rigid mental discipline she had nurtured over the years, devoting her energies to Jake Stalker. Jake was a part of her, an extension of her inner self. She knew how he would react to any given situation, how far he could be pushed by both men and women, his likes and dislikes. He once had cried when his half brother, a young Indian brave, had been slain by a soldier's bullet and the letters to Jeremiah Wade had poured in praising the author for showing such an emotion in Stalker. Throughout the day she had belonged to Jake, but when she turned the key in the workroom door she brushed him from her mind and turned her thoughts to Taylor Shay.

She practically flew to the intercom when it buzzed. "Yes?"

"Dr. Shay to see you, Miss Holland."

"Would you ask him if he'd just like me to come down?"

"Sure, just a minute." There was a pause, then the man said, "Dr. Shay says that's a good idea because he's too weak from hunger to make it up there anyway."

"Tell him to hang on and I'll be right down."

"Better hurry," the man said with a laugh, "he's looking a little shaky."

When Blaze stepped out of the elevator Taylor and the night security guard were deeply engrossed in a discussion about the merits of the New York Giants and the Los Angeles Rams. Blaze was tempted to toss in a comment regarding the attributes of the Jets, but decided that wasn't such a hot idea and instead bid them both a pleasant good evening.

"Hi, Peter Pan," Taylor said. "Don't you think she looks like Peter Pan in that snazzy outfit?" he asked the guard.

"That depends on how she feels about Peter Pan. I haven't been married for forty years for nothing, son. I tread real soft when it comes to women's tempers. No offense, Miss Holland," the man added, grinning at Blaze.

She smiled. "You're a wise man. Dr. Shay is in trouble more often than he's not."

Taylor chuckled. "Ain't that the truth. Good night," he said to the guard. "Remember what I said about the Rams. Next season they'll go all the way, you'll see."

"No, sir, Dr. Shay, nobody can run over my Giants. Good night, folks, have a nice time."

Hadn't anybody ever heard of the New York Jets? Blaze fumed. But she would not open her mouth. If she mentioned the Jets, Taylor would think of the jersey and there was no point in dragging that up again. But the Rams? Was he crazy? For a smart man he sure was dumb!

"What are you scowling about?" he asked as he opened the car door for her.

"I can't stand it! If I don't say something I'll probably pop a blood vessel and die and it'll be all your fault!"

"Huh?"

"The Rams? Taylor, I thought you knew football. Don't you read the papers? Watch TV? Fumble fingers, that's what they are. The Giants are no hotshots either for that matter. I know you don't want to hear about the Jets, but—"

"Excuse me, Howard Cosell, but do you think we could continue this tirade over dinner? I really am hungry."

"Oh, I'm sorry. I guess I got carried away there," she mumbled, getting into the car.

"Is there anything about baseball you'd like to get off your chest?" he asked as he started the car.

"Well, now that you mention it—"

"Oh, please," he moaned. "Enough. The problem is you're right about the football teams and I don't want to hear another word."

"I'm right?" She smiled happily.

"Stow it.'

"Score one for me, Shay."

"Blaze," he said warningly.

"Okay, Okay. What's for dinner?"

It would seem, Blaze decided a half hour later, that just about everything imaginable was for dinner. They had driven down to the Village and managed to find a parking place, bought two large bags full of Chinese food, and were now walking a few short blocks to Taylor's apartment. "We couldn't even pronounce the names of half this stuff, Taylor," she said. "How will we know what we're eating?"

"It doesn't matter. We'll go by how it tastes."

"Suppose it's delicious and then we find out later it's something we hate?"

He chuckled. "That was not one of your brightest statements."

"Made sense to me."

"Well, here we are," he said, climbing the steps of a small brick house. "Are you ready for this?" He opened the front door and she followed him in.

"Looks perfectly normal so far."

"I'll carry the food so in case you faint you won't strew it all over the floor."

He handed her a key and took her bag, then led her

up one flight of stairs and nodded at the door to the front apartment. She unlocked and opened it, then followed his instructions to turn on the light switch just inside the room.

"Oh, my God," she gasped as light flooded the living room. "It's . . . it's pink!"

"Very good," he said. "You figured that out all by yourself."

She walked forward slowly and her eyes grew even wider. The entire place—furniture, carpet, walls, accessories—was decorated in every shade of pink ever created and, she shook her head, a few shades that had been invented just for this nightmare.

"Oh, Taylor, this is simply awful," she said. "How can you stand it?"

"I'm thinking about putting in for Hazardous Duty Pay. Come on." He set the food on a coffee table that was inlaid with pink tiles. "I'll show you the bedroom."

"Oh, no," she said a few moments later when they entered the room. "A canopy bed? You sleep in a pink ruffled canopy bed? I can't believe it. This is hysterical!"

"Do you realize if you came over here in that pink jogging suit you'd blend in so well I might not find you for days?" he said, joining her in uproarious laughter. "I didn't know they made pink refrigerators and stoves, but sure enough they're right out there in the kitchen."

"You poor darling," she said, wrapping her arms around his waist. "I really feel sorry for you. Has anyone else seen this disaster?"

"Only Clare and Bill. They offered to let me bunk with Todd for the semester but I don't fit on a trundle bed. I swore them to secrecy though. My macho image would be shot to hell if anyone knew about this." He buried his face in her hair. "You smell good."

"And you feel divine," she murmured, running her hands up his back.

"Divine?"

"The word for the day."

"Beats 'despicable.' Let's eat."

Sitting cross-legged on the floor by the coffee table, they spread out the food and warily eyed each selection before shrugging and sampling it. Every time Blaze glanced around the room she dissolved in laughter, the infectious throaty sound bringing an instant grin from Taylor. She fell apart again when they entered the tiny kitchen to place the leftover food in the refrigerator, seeing the gleaming pink appliances sparkling against the matching floor.

"I'm exhausted," she finally said, flopping onto the magenta sofa. "I've never laughed so hard in my life."

"What can I say? I told you it was unique."

"That's being polite."

"She must think my apartment in L.A. is really dull."

"What's it like?" Blaze asked. But she didn't want to know, she thought suddenly. She didn't want him to tell her about the world where he really belonged, the one he'd return to in a few months, leaving her here, alone.

"Nothing fancy," he said, "but the furniture is large. You know, big enough for someone my size. I used a lot of the colors you did at your place. I like warm tones—brown, orange, yellow. I think you'd like it."

But she'd never know, would she? she thought miserably. "Sounds lovely," she said softly.

"Say, I almost forgot. I promised you a new nightie and I always keep my word. Sit tight."

Blaze pushed herself up to a sitting position and smiled in delight when Taylor placed a gift-wrapped box on her lap. The paper was lumpy and torn at one corner, the bow dangerously close to falling off. "I wrapped it myself," he said proudly, sitting down next to her.

"Very nice," she said, tugging off the wrinkled paper and lifting the cover of the box. "Oh, Taylor," she whispered, picking up the soft mint green cotton nightshirt. Across the front was the most beautiful butterfly she had ever seen. Done in pastels, it covered the top half of the shirt, the wings appearing almost transparent as the muted colors blended together. "It's beautiful. A butterfly. That's so sweet."

"I told you that your sharing your secret meant a lot to me. I wanted you to know how much."

"Thank you." She clasped her hands behind his neck and pulled him close to her.

Their lips met and, like the butterfly, fluttered softly against each other. Taylor traced the outline of her mouth with his tongue, sending a burning surge of desire deep within her. Sinking his hands into her thick hair he claimed her lips and tongue in an almost rough, frenzied embrace. She sank back against the pillows as she responded in total abandonment. Their breathing became labored and raspy as they continued, hands roving, passions rising to a fever pitch.

"Go try on the nightshirt," he said huskily, close to her lips.

"Yes," was all she managed to say as she got unsteadily to her feet and walked into the bedroom.

Not bothering to shut the door she stripped off her clothes, leaving on only the lacy bikini panties, and drew the nightshirt over her head. It fell to midthigh and the slits on the side exposed the trim on her panties. Her small breasts pushed against the top of the butterfly's wings, making it appear ready for flight.

"Lovely," Taylor said quietly, leaning against the door frame.

"Thank you again for this," she said. Their eyes met, held, sending a message they both understood.

He crossed the room in long, graceful strides, and gathered her into his arms. He kissed her deeply, his lips sensuous and warm as his hands tenderly caressed her. She drank in the feel and aroma of his strong body, etching it indelibly in her mind, storing away in a special space in her heart the vehemence and beauty and strength of the man she was embracing. Boldly she unbuttoned his blue shirt, running her hands over his hair-roughened chest. She heard his sharp intake of breath as she started to loosen his belt buckle, and his hands joined hers to help. Within moments he was naked before her, dark and massive. Leaning over her he helped her off with the nightshirt and steadied her as she removed her panties, then they fell together onto the bed.

Ecstasy. Murmured words of endearment, hands rough then tender, bodies glistening with perspiration as they came together in an explosion of passion that seemed to go on and on and on. Spent at last, they lay together, their breathing slowing, skin cooling, heartbeats quieting but hands still resting on each other in comfortable possessiveness.

"We went there again, Taylor," Blaze said softly, "to our private world. It's ours. No one else knows where it is or that it even exists. Only you can take me there."

"And I can't go without you," he said, brushing her hair away from her face with his large hand. "It's a mini-miracle every time we make love."

"Mini?"

"The true miracle is the creation of a child, a new life. But what we have is rare and beautiful, so very special; to me, it's a small miracle within itself every time you come to me."

"You're going to make me cry, Taylor."

"You can't. Don't you know that in the state of New York it's against the law to cry after having made love in a pink-ruffled canopy bed?"

"Really?"

"Yep. You'll end up in the clink."

"Heaven forbid. I guess I won't blubber then."

"Good."

"I think I'm hungry."

"It's all in your imagination, Blaze. You've heard somewhere that when you eat Chinese food you want something more an hour later and you believed it."

"I'm really not hungry?"

"Nope."

"Then why is my stomach growling?"

"Let's see." He pressed his ear against her stomach. "Son of a gun, you're right. Put your butterfly on and we'll cook up an omelet."

They tossed some of the leftover food into the foamy egg batter and fried it to a golden brown, only to decide it tasted absolutely terrible. They settled for cereal and then lingered over coffee, chatting in the small, pink kitchen.

"I guess," Taylor said finally, "I had better get you home."

"Now?"

"It's late and as much as I want you to stay with me tonight it's not a great idea."

"Why not? I even have a nightie."

"Which you definitely would not need. But I have a department meeting tomorrow before my first class, which means I'll be getting up practically in the middle of the night."

"So?"

"So, I'm not leaving you here alone and it's dumb to drag you out that early."

"I can take a taxi later."

"No. In case you didn't notice this isn't the best

neighborhood in the world. It's rough down here and I'm not letting you stay by yourself."

"Not letting . . . Now wait a minute, Taylor."

"Blaze, we can argue for the next hour and you can pull a feminist routine on me but I won't change my mind. I will not—do you get that?—will not allow you to stay here. Now, go get dressed and I'll take you home."

Blaze opened her mouth, shut it, shook her head, and got up from the table. "I do believe," she said, "that I'll go get my clothes on and then perhaps, since it's getting so late, you should take me back to my apartment."

"Makes sense. I'm glad you thought of it."

His deep chuckle as she walked from the room was quickly muffled by the pink throw pillow that hit Taylor squarely in the nose.

"I'm not going to be able to see you tomorrow, Blaze," Taylor said later, after she was dressed and clasped in his arms in her living room.

"Why? Tomorrow's Sunday. Surely you don't have classes."

"I'm so far behind on my work it's a crime. I have papers to grade, an exam to make up, and a lecture to write. It would seem, you see, there's this beautiful Indian princess who has come into my life and thrown me totally off schedule."

"You mean I'm the cause of the downfall of your career?"

"Among other things."

"What does that mean?"

"Skip it. But seriously, I've got to burn the midnight oil, as the saying goes, and get caught up. I'll call you, though."

"Better than nothing. Don't you have your class lectures already prepared from other years?"

"This is something else entirely. I'm a guest

speaker for a lecture series some organization is sponsoring."

"No kidding? Can I come and hear you?"

"If you want to, I suppose, but it's not that big a deal."

"Of course I want to. I bet Uncle Ben would too."

"Well, it's sold out but I'll see if I can get you a couple of tickets."

"Sold out! And you stand there saying it's no big deal? Weren't you even going to tell me about it?"

"In all honesty, it never crossed my mind. I do this stuff all the time, Blaze. It's not my debut or anything. Don't get so crabby."

"Damn it, half of New York is going to be there and here I would have sat not knowing a thing."

"Five hundred people would be a little closer to the number." He smiled. "Okay, I'll find two tickets someplace, but I won't be able to see you afterward because I'll be tied up with the press and—"

"The press!"

"Is there an echo in this room?"

"Taylor Shay, you make me so mad!"

"That's not news."

"You promise to get the tickets?"

"On my honor and hope to die, or however you say that."

"Okay."

"Now may I kiss you good night?"

"Of course, silly man."

"You know that gray hair I wanted so I'd look distinguished?"

"Yes."

"Somehow I get the feeling it's on its way."

Six

"Good morning, Uncle Ben," Blaze said cheerfully when he telephoned the next morning.

"Tell me you're still seeing Taylor Shay," Ben said.

"I'm still seeing Taylor Shay."

"Good."

"Why?"

"Because he's giving a lecture tomorrow night and I just found out there are no tickets left. If anyone can get us in it's Taylor himself."

"Say no more, it's as good as done. Taylor promised he'd get seats for both of us. I didn't know it was that soon, though. He never really said when it was."

"Great. I meant to take care of it but I was working and the days got away from me. By the time I checked it was sold out. Are you meeting him afterward?"

"No, he said he'd be in a press conference."

"Doesn't surprise me. He's very sought after by the

media. I'll tell you what, I'll take you for a late dinner to The Russian Tea Room after the lecture."

"Whew. Ritzy."

"If you get me into that lecture, I'll be in such a fine mood I'll buy you two desserts."

"Great. You've got a date."

" 'Bye, Blaze."

"Good-bye, sweet Uncle."

Blaze hung up the phone and rested her head on the top of the sofa. She had been so busy yelling at Taylor for not telling her about the lecture, she'd forgotten to ask him when it was. Tomorrow night. Wait a minute! He had to work all day and he'd be tied up after the speech. . . . That was two days without seeing him. "Well, damn," she said aloud.

"Problem?" Murphy asked, pausing by the sofa with a cup of coffee in her hand. Blaze had asked her to come in that morning for a few hours to finish up the New Mexico research.

"Then he'll teach the whole next day," Blaze continued, "so that's actually three. But so what? I'm a totally independent woman. It doesn't matter. When he shows, he shows. I have my own life to lead, plenty to do. Right, Murphy?"

"Did I miss something here?"

"It's just that I've grown . . . accustomed to having him around. Do you know what I mean? But it's not as if I'm going to pine away or anything. It just came as a surprise that the lecture is tomorrow night. Lord knows the man has to get his speech written or—"

"What are you talking about?" Murphy yelled.

"Murphy, sometimes I think you don't listen to a word I say," Blaze said as she stomped out of the room.

"Give me patience," Murphy moaned, rolling her eyes to the heavens.

"I sure wish it was football season," Blaze said, retracing her steps. "Oh boy, would I love to see his face when those Rams get creamed. Speaking of that gorgeous face, Murphy, if I'm so independent why am I miserable that it will be three days before I see it? Don't answer that, I don't even want to think about the answer. Come on, let's get to work."

"I'm too old for this," Murphy mumbled, as she followed Blaze into the workroom. "I'm losing my mind, I'm sure of it. My brain is dissolving and they'll cart me away."

"Murphy, are you all right?"

"One of us is crazy, Blaze, but let's not vote on who it is. I'm going to concentrate on Jake and blot you from my consciousness."

"Huh?"

"Ignore me, I'm close to hysteria."

"Guess what? Taylor is giving a lecture and I'm going with Uncle Ben."

"Maybe I'll see you there."

"You have a ticket?"

"Sure. I got it the minute they went on sale. I just assumed you'd be attending."

"Brother, the whole world knew about it except me. That makes me so damn mad. Hey, want to see the nightie Taylor bought me?"

"What I want is a sedative but, yes, show me the nightie. How is the good Professor, by the way?"

"Fine. He took me to his house last night but I can't tell you what it looks like or he'd break my neck. It's not really his though, so it's not his fault."

"I'm going over the edge."

"Murphy, you like Taylor, don't you?"

"Yes, Blaze, I do. There's a certain quality about him, a depth, that there hasn't been in the other men you've dated. Taylor is . . . well, I'm sure I don't have to tell you."

"No, you don't. He's very special," Blaze said quietly. "Very, very special."

"And?"

"Do you have the rest of that research on New Mexico?"

"Okay, Blaze, we'll play this your way. I'll get the material."

Taylor sounded tired when he telephoned just after ten that night and Blaze felt sorry for him when he said he still had several more hours of work ahead of him.

"You shouldn't push so hard," she said.

"It's my own fault. I let things slide. Oh, you're all set for the lecture tomorrow night. I left your name at the ticket office at the main entrance. There's a seat for Ben too."

"Thank you, Taylor. Uncle Ben said to tell you how much he appreciates it. He was very upset when he found out it was sold out. We're looking forward to hearing you speak."

"You'll give me a big head. Say, how's our butterfly?"

"Soft and warm and . . . lonely."

"Oh, Blaze, you're killing me. You're sitting in it right now, aren't you?"

"Yes, I am," she said, looking down at the nightshirt.

"And you smell good because you just had a bath."

"Lilacs. I used lilac soap."

"Do you think it will snow?"

"What?"

"We're talking about the weather now. The way that conversation was going I was about to come pounding on your door."

"Do you really have to finish all that work tonight?"

"Yes. But, Blaze, I miss you. I wish I was there right now. I'd—Damn it. Just say, 'I miss you, Taylor. Good night.' "

"I miss you, Taylor, but—"

"Good night, Blaze."

"Taylor? Oh, darn it anyway," she said to the dial tone, before slamming the receiver into place.

This was nuts, she thought as she crossed her arms over her breasts. You'd think he was being shipped overseas, maybe never to return from the horrors of war. She'd just seen the man the night before and she'd see him again tomorrow. She and five hundred other people, for heaven's sake. He sounded so tired. Had he remembered to eat dinner? There sure wasn't much food in that stupid pink refrigerator. A man his size needed a lot of nourishment. If he were here she could fix him a decent meal. If he were here he would take her in his arms and hold her and those wonderful lips would kiss her until she—"Good grief," she said, shaking her head. "I wonder if it will snow?"

Blaze was unusually subdued the next day and Murphy treaded softly, aware that her friend was deep in thought. When the atmosphere hadn't changed by lunch time, however, she became concerned that Blaze wasn't feeling up to par.

"You're awfully quiet today, kiddo," Murphy said. "Anything wrong?"

"What? Oh, no, not really. I've just been thinking about . . . Murphy, do I seem different to you?"

"Like what?"

"Older? More mature?"

"That's a tough question, Blaze."

"I can't get Taylor out of my mind. You know, wondering if he's eating right, getting enough rest, stuff like that. He's not used to these winters after all those years in California and he might not dress warmly enough."

"And?"

"It doesn't make sense to me. He's a grown man who's perfectly capable of taking care of himself. He certainly doesn't need me worrying about him. So, I'm wondering if maybe some biological time clock has gone off inside me, triggering my mothering instincts."

"You think your concern for Taylor is an inner desire to be a mother?"

"What else could it be? When I was dating the football player, the guy could have been killed out there on any given Sunday, but I never gave it a thought. This is very confusing. I'm really trying to get in touch with myself but I don't seem to be able to make it add up."

"That's because you're afraid of what you'll find out, Blaze," Murphy said quietly.

"What do you mean?"

"Oh, Blaze, don't you see? You're not suffering from some nutty urge to have a baby. Damn it, Blaze, you're in love with Taylor Shay! Head over heels, totally off the wall in love."

"I am not!"

"Then what would you call it? Do you cherish every minute you're together? Miss him when you're separated? Do you feel a warm glow when he walks into the room and fall apart when he touches you?"

"Yes, but—"

"Then face it. It's happened, Blaze, in spite of your lofty ideals and Godawful arrangement to stay detached and in charge. You're in love, Blaze Holland, and there's not a darn thing you can do to change it."

"No, Murphy, you're wrong. I—"

"I'm right and you know I am. The next thing you'd better figure out is what you're going to do about it."

"Do?"

"You and Taylor have a pact. If one of you breaks the rules of the game, it's over. You fouled out. You're benched. You don't get to play anymore."

"What?"

"Hey, you two drew up the ground rules, not me. You said if one of you lost control of his or her emotions, then the relationship had to end. You, like it or not, are definitely out of control."

"No! Oh, granted he's come to mean more to me than anyone I've ever known, but I am not in love with him. I refuse to be. You have to want to fall in love to fall in love and since I have no desire to fall in love then I'm not in love. Understand? This discussion is over! I'm going for a walk." Blaze marched from the room.

"Oh, Blaze," Murphy said softly, shaking her head. "It's too late, don't you see? Taylor Shay came, saw, and conquered. You're a goner."

Blaze pushed her hands deep into the pockets of her red parka and walked along, her boots hitting the pavement in heavy, angry strides. Murphy was all off base about this, she thought frantically. It couldn't have happened to her without her knowledge. She cared for Taylor, she wasn't denying that, but *love* him? *In* love with him? No! That would mean forever, for the rest of her life. He was going to leave in June and she'd be left here with a broken heart and an empty bed. That's what it was, actually. Sex. The most beautiful, wonderful sexual encounter of her limited experience. Just because she had a fantastic lover didn't mean she was in love with the lover who made love so—"Oh, damn it," she yelled, quickly following with an, "Excuse me, ma'am," as an elderly woman glared sternly at her.

Blaze stopped walking and saw with surprise that her wandering had brought her to Tilly's Tearoom. With a sigh she entered the fragrant establishment and sank into a chair at one of the small tables. Tilly raised a curious eyebrow at Blaze's sullen expression. She plunked a cup of tea in front of Blaze, then made sure the customers at the counter were all taken care of before joining the younger woman.

"Now," Tilly said, when she sat down across from Blaze, "what's up?"

"I am not in love with Taylor Shay," Blaze said fiercely.

"Oh? Who are we convincing here, you or me?"

"It's a plain and simple fact."

"I see. Then why the hypertension?"

"I just had a go round with Murphy about this. She's made up her mind that I'm—"

"Never known Murphy to make snap judgments. There must be something behind her observation."

"I've admitted that Taylor is an important part of my days—"

"And nights?"

"Oh, all right," Blaze snapped, "and my nights but—"

"And you feel his presence when he isn't there, wonder what he's doing, count the hours until he holds you? Your bed suddenly seems too large to sleep in alone and you worry that he might forget to wear his coat."

"How did you know I was . . . I mean . . ."

"Blaze, you're in love with Taylor Shay," Tilly said firmly.

"What is this? A conspiracy? It really makes me so

angry that everyone is sitting around deciding how I feel about him."

"Well, it doesn't take a fancy college degree to figure it out. Why don't you just admit it's true?"

"I will not! In the first place, I'm not in love with him. Secondly, supposing, just supposing, that I was, it would mean I would never see him again."

"Why not?"

"Because Taylor and I agreed that if one of us fell in love with the other the whole thing would be over. He has no desire to make a commitment and wants no part of a serious relationship."

"I see. Apparently you've thoroughly discussed this."

"Absolutely. He felt there was this remote chance he might develop strong feelings for me and he doesn't intend to let that happen."

"He said that?"

"Right from his mouth."

"Well, then he must be dating other women, right?"

"Oh, no. He said he wouldn't share me, so we're only seeing each other."

"Interesting." Tilly nodded. "Did he put a time limit on this affair?"

"He's here on sabbatical. He'll be going back to California in June."

"So you're just his New York City fling."

"Tilly, what a horrible thing to say! What Taylor and I have togther is the most wonderful—" Blaze frowned. "Forget it."

"Was Taylor the one who first brought up the possibility of something serious happening between you two?"

"Yes."

"And then you, I presume, told him very loudly you

wanted no part of the love bug bit, and after that the rules were drawn up?"

"Yes."

"Oh my, I do want to meet this boy. Tricky fellow, very tricky. When are you going to bring him around?"

"Tilly, what are you babbling about?"

"Of course, I'll get to see what he looks like when he lectures tonight but I want him here in the flesh."

"You're going to hear him speak too?"

"Wouldn't miss it for the world."

"I can't believe this. I'm going home." Blaze got up from her chair.

"Remember, Blaze, I want Taylor's tush right here at this table. As for you, you're playing games with yourself and it's going to catch up with you."

"Games?"

"Oh, honey," Tilly said, her voice softening, "you're running and there's nowhere to hide. What's done is done. It's time you faced that."

"No! You and Murphy are wrong! Good-bye, Tilly," Blaze said, and left the shop.

"Yes, indeed." Tilly smiled to herself. "I surely do want to meet Taylor Shay."

Blaze refused to think during the chilly walk back to her apartment and instead counted the cracks in the sidewalk. Murphy was just locking the door to the workroom as Blaze arrived. "Murphy," she said, "I'm sorry I was such a shrew. I didn't mean to yell at you."

"No problem. You have a lot on your mind."

"You worked all weekend. Why don't you take a couple days off."

"Okay. Let's see, this is Monday. I'll come in early Thursday, all right?"

"Sure."

"In the meantime if you just want to talk, give me a call."

"Thanks, but I'm fine. Really."

"Whatever you say. 'Bye for now."

"Good-bye."

Blaze ate three peanut butter sandwiches with accompanying glasses of milk, deciding she would die of starvation if she didn't eat before the late dinner with Uncle Ben. After a long bath she brushed her hair until her arms ached and then pulled on a burnt orange wool dress that accentuated her dark coloring beautifully.

She was pretty and smart, had a marvelous career and oodles of money, she thought, gazing at her reflection in the mirror. What more did she need? Nothing.

She pressed her fingertips against her lips, remembering Taylor's kiss, and a burning sensation started deep within her and spread through her entire body until her cheeks were flushed and warm. "No!" she shouted to the empty room. "I do not love him! I am not in love with Taylor Shay!"

"Ready, Blaze?" Ben asked when she answered his knock at the door a few minutes later.

"All set." She smiled. "Goodness, you look handsome. You'll have to beat the women off with a stick."

"You like this?" He smoothed down the jacket of his dark brown suit. "Taylor will steal my thunder, though, the minute he steps on stage. He's a handsome fellow, don't you think?"

"I hadn't noticed."

"Oh, hell, is it going to be one of those nights when you disagree with everything I say? I suppose you haven't observed his pearly-gray eyes or athletic build either?"

"Not particularly."

"I used to swat your rear end when you were little and I caught you in a lie, young lady. Now all I can do is stand here and worry about an ulcer. Let's go, you're giving me a headache."

Blaze waited in the lobby of the large auditorium while Ben picked up their tickets. She was surrounded by a very mixed group of people, from older women in furs to college students in jeans, all hurrying to their seats.

"Here," Ben said when he returned. "Taylor left a message for you."

Blaze opened the folded piece of paper and read, "Blaze: Being an absentminded Professor, if I don't see you tonight I'll forget what you look like. Please meet me in Room Seven backstage after the lecture. I'll have ten minutes in which to plant numerous kisses on your lovely lips. Taylor."

Blaze smiled happily. "He wants to see me after his speech, Room Seven backstage, but only for ten minutes. Do you mind waiting?"

"Of course not," Ben said. "Let's find our places."

They made their way down the aisle, both amazed that they had two of the best seats in the house. "I don't see how he got a hold of these," Ben said. "He must have shot the people who had these tickets."

Blaze laughed. "Who knows?"

Within minutes the lights dimmed slightly and a man obviously in charge of the lecture series stepped up to the microphone. He thanked everyone present for their patronage, then went on to list the credits of that evening's speaker. After a roar of applause, Taylor took his place at the microphone.

Taylor—big, strong, wonderful Taylor looked devastatingly handsome in a three-piece charcoal gray suit, his thick hair falling just to the collar of the jacket and combed over his ears. Blaze's heart raced at the sight of him.

"Isn't he scrumptious?" the woman behind her

whispered to her companion. "Wouldn't you love to see him in a bathing suit?"

"Forget the suit," another woman said. "Let's go for a centerfold."

Sorry, sister, Blaze thought smugly, that body is taken.

Taylor's deep, rich voice filled the auditorium. He began his lecture with the explanation he'd given Blaze earlier about his concern for historical accuracy in fiction. Again she heard the determination in his voice, could see heads nodding in approval, and she swelled with pride.

"It has been my privilege since coming to your city," Taylor continued, "to meet Benjamin Kiowa. Mr. Kiowa has dedicated his life to presenting the true facts about the Indian people of this nation and their place in our history. If only there were more men of Mr. Kiowa's caliber and integrity among us."

"How about that?" Blaze whispered.

"I'll be damned," Ben said, a wide smile on his face.

"There are, however," Taylor went on, "some authors who have abused their right to take pen in hand. One of those foremost in my mind tonight is Jeremiah Wade."

"What?" Blaze gasped.

"Quiet," Ben said, grabbing her hand.

"I have followed Mr. Wade's career with interest since the first Jake Stalker novel was published several years ago," Taylor said, "and have found him to be an excellent writer with an apparent dedication to proper research. Until now."

"What is he talking about?" Blaze hissed.

"Shhh."

"In Jeremiah Wade's last book," Taylor said, holding a copy for all to see, "Jake Stalker crossed over into Mexico in the year 1860, where he encountered a group of desperadoes intent on ravishing a young American woman."

"Right," Blaze said.

"Jake saved the woman by pulling from the boot of his saddle a Winchester Rifle, with which he skillfully drove the bandits into the hills."

"So what's the problem?" Blaze whispered.

Ben scowled. "Shut up and listen."

"Ladies and gentlemen," Taylor said, leaning forward on the podium, "Jake Stalker could not have wielded a Winchester Rifle on that day in 1860. Oliver Fisher Winchester didn't invent that gun until 1866. Jake may have had the Henry Rifle that was produced in 1857 by Mr. Winchester, but it is totally impossible and falsely presented to you, the public, to say that that man saved the life of a woman with a weapon that did not exist!"

"Oh, my God," Blaze said, her hands flying to her mouth. "I couldn't have made that kind of mistake. I—"

"Blaze, if you won't be quiet I'm going to drag you out of here," Ben said.

"Although I have never met Mr. Wade," Taylor said, "I send this message to him. Take stock of the responsibility you hold. Granted, this is one small error in numerous volumes but it is an error of negligence and carelessness. If such carelessness continues, I fear Mr. Wade will make larger, more critical errors in the future. I will be closely scrutinizing Jake Stalker's every action in forthcoming books."

A wave of icy misery swept over Blaze and she felt frozen in place, unable to breathe. Taylor moved on to other authors, criticizing and praising as the situation warranted, but she couldn't concentrate on what he was saying.

What has he done? her mind screamed. He would destroy her, crush the career she'd worked so hard and long to establish. He'd presented her as a sloppy, inept writer who didn't care enough to do proper research. It was slander. Grossly unfair. How could he do this? One mistake. One small slip and he'd ripped her apart. Damn him, she'd—

Thundering noise broke into her anguished thoughts as the audience enthusiastically applauded Taylor. He smiled, nodded his thanks, and strode from the stage. The house lights came up to full power and Blaze blinked against the sudden glare. Numbly she felt Ben pull her to her feet and steer her down the aisle toward the stage.

"Wait," she said suddenly, as if coming out of a trance, "where are we going?"

"You're supposed to meet Taylor backstage, remember?"

"No!" She came to a complete halt, only to be jerked nearly off her feet as Ben pulled her to the edge of the stage and out of the surging crowd.

"Now you listen to me," he said, taking her by the shoulders. "You're going back there and will smile or kiss him or do whatever he would normally expect."

"I can't! God, Uncle Ben, didn't you hear what he said about me? I—"

"No! I heard what he said about Jeremiah Wade. And, Blaze, he was right. Damn it, I've drummed research into your head until I was blue in the face. You were six years off on that rifle. Six years! There's no excuse for that. None."

"But—"

"I'm going with you to see Taylor and so help me if you aren't sunshine itself I'm going to whop your tail end. Now march, young lady, and bear in mind I have an eye on you. Six years. Stalker shot a rifle that wasn't invented for another six years. Blaze, I could shake you until your teeth rattle. Come on."

With her mind whirling Blaze followed Ben backstage. He rapped sharply on the door to Room Seven, and Taylor opened it instantly.

"Blaze, Ben," he said, smiling. "Quick, come in. I'm hiding out for a minute in here."

"Fine speech, Taylor," Ben said. "Thanks for the seats. I enjoyed myself immensely."

"You're welcome. I hope you didn't mind my reference to your work."

"Mind? Lord, no. You kicked my reputation up the ladder a notch or two. I appreciate it. Listen, I know it's Blaze you want to see so pretend I'm not here. I escorted her back because there was such a crowd out there. Haul her over to the other side of the room and do whatever's on your mind."

"Thanks, Ben." Taylor took Blaze's hand and led her to a far corner of the small room. "Hello, pretty lady," he said softly. "You look like a delicious carrot in that orange dress."

"Hello, Taylor," she said, gazing at the floor.

"Hey, what's wrong?" he asked, tilting her chin up. "I'm sorry I didn't call you today but—"

"I know you were busy. I understand."

"Then what is it?"

"Nothing."

"Come on, Blaze, don't hand me that. You're obviously upset and I want to know why," he said, his voice growing louder.

"Taylor, please." Blaze glanced quickly at Ben, who frowned back at her.

"I'll get through with the reporters as soon as I can and come over," Taylor said. "We'll talk."

"No, I won't be there. Uncle Ben and I are going out to dinner."

"Actually," Ben said, "I'm rather tired. I'll have to give you a raincheck on that dinner, Blaze. She'll be home, Taylor. Okay, I'm invisible again."

"Then it's settled," Taylor said. "I'll be there as soon as possible."

"I really don't think we have anything to—"

"Hold it just a damn minute," Taylor roared, his jaw tightening. "Something has got you all in a dither and it's obviously directed at me. We're getting to the bottom of this if it takes all night. I—"

"Dr. Shay," a man said, poking his head into the room, "the reporters are waiting."

"I'll be right there."

"Taylor—"

"Later, Blaze." Taylor walked away from her, shook Ben's hand, and left.

"Well," Ben said, a wide smile on his face, "now I understand." He stepped away from the wall and walked over to Blaze.

"What does that mean?" she said, sinking wearily into a chair.

"Remember last year when that critic wrote that scathing review on Jake Stalker? He said if Jake made love as often as Jeremiah Wade had him drop his pants, Jake would be too weak to sit in the saddle. I felt it was a very unfair piece but you laughed so hard I thought you'd pass out."

"So?"

"So, Taylor Shay's criticism of your work is justified, but here you are, mad as hell. Or so I thought."

"You're not making any sense," she said tersely.

"Oh, but I am. You're not angry, Blaze, you're hurt. This was Taylor criticizing you, telling the world you made a mistake. And that cuts you to the quick because, my beautiful Indian maiden, you are very deeply in love with one Dr. Taylor Shay."

"Oh, no, you don't!" she shrieked, leaping to her feet. "No you don't, don't, don't! You all got together, didn't you? You, Tilly, Murphy—you had a little meeting regarding the emotional status of Blaze Holland's heart! Well, you three can take a header off the Empire State Building because I'm not buying it. I am not, for the one millionth time today, in love with Taylor Shay!"

"Okay." Ben shrugged, grinning broadly.

"That's it? Just, 'Okay'? I don't trust you, Benjamin Kiowa. What are you up to?"

"Me? I'm just the guy who's paying for the taxi that's about to take us home."

"And that's another thing. Just what in the hell happened to my fancy dinner at The Russian Tea Room?"

"I told you, I'm tired."

"Ha! You can run circles around me and you know it. You're dumping me right into Taylor's lap."

"You can always camp out in Central Park if you don't want to see him."

"Don't talk to me."

"By the way, Blaze, how are you going to explain to Taylor why you're so upset without telling him you're Jeremiah Wade?"

"I have no idea," she said stiffly.

"Didn't think you did. Know something? You're in a real mess. You've either got to concoct a story to justify your lousy mood or tell him the truth."

"The truth? But you said that no one should know that I'm—"

"Now, Blaze, I can hardly expect you to keep something as important as this from the man you love."

"I told you! I am not—"

"Ah, yes, I forgot. Well, I sure wish I could hide in a corner and see how you wiggle your way out of this one, but I'm afraid you're on your own. Let's go home."

"Well, darn it, I'm hungry."

"You're about to face a major crisis in your life and you're hungry?"

"I can't think straight on an empty stomach."

"I told Taylor you'd be home and that's where you're going. Eat something when you get there."

"You're a crummy date."

"Tough."

"Murphy was here tonight, Uncle Ben. She's going to be upset by what Taylor said about Jeremiah Wade too."

"She'll be all right. She's probably wondering what you're going to say to Taylor, just like I am. Come on, Blaze, it's time to face the music."

A bitter cold, driving rain greeted them as they left the warmth of the building and dashed for a waiting taxi. Blaze shivered and snuggled close to Ben in the back seat, where he wrapped his arm protectively around her shoulders.

"Oh, Blaze," he said softly, "sometimes it's hard for me to realize you're all grown up. I want to step in and protect you, make sure you don't get hurt. It was so easy when you were a little girl but now, well, I have to turn my back and walk away. You're a woman and you're dealing with problems that are none of my business."

"So much has changed since I met Taylor, Uncle Ben. There's a part of me that wishes he'd never left California and another that is so glad he's come into my life. I hate being confused. I just hate it. Everything was so simple before."

"I wish I could tell you everything between you and Taylor is going to work out just fine, but I don't know that for a fact and I've never lied to you. I'll just be here in the wings if you need me."

"Thank you, Uncle Ben."

"Don't forget to eat when you get home. When

Taylor arrives I have the feeling you're going to need all the mental energies you can muster."

"He looks about eight feet tall when he's mad."

"But handsome."

"Oh, yes, always handsome." She laughed softly, wishing she was ten years old and Uncle Ben would be tucking her safely into bed in a few minutes.

The wind and rain beat against the taxi as it wove through the bustling traffic. She wondered if Taylor had remembered to carry an umbrella.

Seven

Blaze tugged off the pretty orange dress as soon as she entered her bedroom. The storm had increased its intensity and she and Ben had been drenched as they dashed from the taxi to the apartment building. He had kissed her gently on the cheek before she stepped out of the elevator at her floor, and she had managed a weak smile in return.

Dressed in jeans and a bright purple sweatshirt, she wandered into the kitchen and searched for something to eat in the refrigerator. Settling for three bananas and two cartons of yogurt, she ate her strange meal without tasting it and then sat on the sofa with her hands clasped tightly in her lap.

It was like waiting outside the principal's office, she thought dismally. No, it was worse than that. She was Marie Antoinette, and everyone knew what had happened to her. She should never have seen Taylor after the lecture. She needed time to calm down, think rationally. So, okay, now she was calm—

Damn it! Why did he have to pick on Jeremiah Wade? A teeny-tiny little six year goof-up and Professor Shay went berserk! She had been so proud of her work, felt that Taylor would respect her for her careful research if he knew she had created Jake Stalker. But now he was hot on the trail of Jeremiah Wade, waiting and watching for the man to make another mistake. Uncle Ben was right, she was more hurt than angry. Taylor had maligned her. No, now wait a minute, not her exactly, Jeremiah Wade. But she was Jeremiah and— "Oh, Lord," she shrieked, as the intercom's buzz startled her out of her thoughts.

"Dr. Shay, Miss Holland," the guard said, when she answered the intercom.

"Fine." I guess. Oh, now what? She'd smile, that's what she'd do. One nice big, toothy grin and he'd forget she was in a rotten mood earlier and she wouldn't have to try to explain what was wrong with her. Good plan. She was all set, she decided firmly, reaching for the doorknob as Taylor's knock sounded, a wide, rigid smile plastered across her face.

"Hi," she said brightly, only to gasp as Taylor strode past her into the room. "What happened to you? You're dripping wet."

"Some dope forgot to reserve me a parking place and I had to walk seven blocks to my car in that rain." He pulled off his soggy overcoat. "Damn, I'm cold."

"You've got to get out of those clothes. You're soaked through."

"Later," he said, turning to face her. "We talk, then take off our clothes providing the conversation goes right. First a carrot, now a grape," he added, eyeing the purple sweatshirt. "You're amazing."

"Do you want a drink to warm you up? I really wish

you'd get out of those clammy things. You're going to get sick."

"Don't worry about it. Yeah, I'll have a drink and then you're going to tell me what in the hell is the matter with you." His shoes squished with water as he walked to the sofa. "I guess I can't sit on your furniture."

"Go ahead, it'll dry." She poured him a brandy and handed it to him.

"Ugh," he said, after taking a swallow. "Burns my throat."

"See? You're getting sick." She sat down beside him on the sofa.

"Blaze, talk to me. What happened since I saw you last?"

"Nothing. I was just a little surprised at your speech, that's all."

"The lecture? Because I mentioned Ben? You heard him say he was pleased with—"

"No, what you said about Uncle Ben was very nice. It was . . . the others. I guess I didn't know you were going to be so . . . brutal."

"What? Because I called them on the carpet for sloppy writing and inadequate research? Come on, you're overreacting."

"Overreacting?" she yelled, jumping to her feet. "Do you have any notion what it takes someone like Jeremiah Wade, for example, to produce a Jake Stalker novel? Do you? There's hours and hours of hard work and tedious attention to detail and—"

"What are you?" he roared. "A one woman groupie of Jeremiah Wade's? The man blew it. Stalker shot a rifle that hadn't been invented! If telling Wade that was junky work then, okay, color me brutal. Are we finished with this yet?"

"No! Have you any idea what you've done? You damaged a man's career, a career built on years of dedicated work. It wasn't fair, Taylor. You—Good heavens," she said, as he suddenly started coughing so hard he seemed to be having difficulty catching his breath.

"Boy," he said when the fit ended, "that hurt."

Blaze looked at him anxiously. That hoarse cough hadn't sounded good. "Taylor, take off your clothes."

"Not yet. You've accused me of not being fair and I intend to defend myself. I gave Wade credit for being a good writer. I simply warned him to watch his step in the future and not get careless again."

"You bully!" she shrieked. "How dare you threaten him like that. You'll get him so shook up he'll probably get writer's block and be ruined."

"Something isn't right here," Taylor said, rubbing his forehead. "Why do you care so much? You work for Benjamin Kiowa, who is excellent, first rate. I'd think you'd be glad to get the riffraff cleared out of the ranks."

"The what? How dare you call me . . . him . . . Jeremiah . . . Mr. Wade . . . Damn you!"

"What did you say?" Taylor asked, his eyes wide.

"Nothing."

"You said, 'me.' I heard you. What in the hell is going on here? If I didn't know better I'd think you were Jeremiah—my God, Blaze, is that what this is all about? Are you Jeremiah Wade? Did you write those Jake Stalker books?"

"Yes! Yes, damn it, yes!" she screamed, fighting back her tears. "And you're trying to crucify me! One mistake. One! And the mighty Dr. Shay takes it upon himself to act as judge and jury and pronounce Jeremiah Wade guilty of disregard of history. What's my sentence, Professor? Am I to be hanged by the neck until dead?"

"You lied to me?" he whispered. "You pretended to

be your uncle's assistant and the whole time you were . . . You lied?"

"No. I mean, no one knows that I'm really . . . it has to be a secret." She was suddenly confused by the direction the heated argument had taken.

"A secret from me? Me? After what we've come to have together? What we've shared? A secret, even though we know about the toast and the butterflies? We're talking about your life, who you are and what you do, and you couldn't tell me?"

"Taylor, I—"

"Everything is a game to you, isn't it, Blaze?" he said, getting to his feet, his jaw set in a tight, angry line. "You just switch around from one identity to another as the mood strikes. Where do I fit into the picture? Or is my role limited strictly to the bedroom?"

"That's a rotten thing to say!"

"I don't understand you, Blaze. I thought I did, but I was very wrong. Don't expect me to apologize for what I said about Jeremiah Wade." He picked up his coat and walked to the door. "After all, I really don't know who in the hell he is or what makes him tick, now do I?"

"Taylor, wait, I—"

"Good-bye, Blaze. Tell Ben it was nice to have met him."

Taylor slammed the door behind him with such force the crystal cover of the hurricane lamp rattled precariously on its base. Blaze took a sharp, shuddering breath and then gave way to sobs that racked her body as she stumbled down the hall and flung herself across the big bed.

He was gone. Taylor had walked out of her living room and her life. Forever. She hadn't lied. She'd just withheld some information. No, she'd lied. It was true. But she'd had to. She couldn't have told him she was Jeremiah Wade. Why not? After all, she loved him so much and—

"What?" she shrieked, sitting bolt upright on the bed. "What did I say? I love Taylor Shay? I do? Oh, God, yes. Yes, I do with my whole heart and mind and soul and body and whatever else I left out—and I'm never going to see him again!"

The tears flowed through the long lonely night until, at last exhausted, she slept. She was curled in a ball in the middle of the bed, huddled against the cold, without the energy to pull the spread over her. The shrill ringing of the telephone woke her from her restless slumber and she reached for it automatically, then stopped. The clock on the nightstand read nearly noon, and Blaze shook her head to dispel the cobwebs of sleep while the telephone continued its insistent summons.

She didn't want to talk to anyone, she thought, staring blankly at the screaming instrument until it finally, blessedly, gave up. Uncle Ben would want to know what had happened last night. Murphy would be anxious about her reaction to the lecture. And the worst part was knowing that no matter how many times she answered the phone, it would never be Taylor's voice she'd hear.

With a sigh she pulled off her clothes and showered, then dressed in blue corduroy pants and a blue ski sweater that had a snow-covered mountain and pine trees across the front. The blue down jacket she pulled out of the closet felt as heavy as her gloomy mood and, ignoring the once more ringing telephone, she left the apartment.

Having no desire to see Tilly, or anyone else for that matter, she walked slowly in the opposite direction from the tearoom, her mind filled with the image of

Taylor Shay. It would have been over anyway, she thought, trying desperately to console her aching heart. She had broken the rules and fallen in love with him. She wouldn't have been able to hide that from him now that she knew, and he would have walked away. But he might have kissed her good-bye, made love to her one more time, departed quietly, gently, leaving her memories intact. Now all she could see was the anger and hurt that had been written on his face the night before. My God, he hated her, despised her for not sharing her greatest secret. But she hadn't known she loved him, hadn't known she had the luxury of lying in his arms and telling him of her accomplishments as Jeremiah Wade. And now it was too late. But anyway she looked at it, she'd lose. If he could ever forgive her he'd find out she loved him, and he'd disappear. But he wouldn't forgive her. She'd seen the pain in his eyes, the distrust. It was over. Taylor Shay was gone.

On she walked, her mind replaying the dreadful, torturous scenario over and over until her head ached and her legs felt wooden from the hours of trudging along the cold pavement. A clock in a store window told her it was nearly five and since she felt light-headed from lack of food, she made her way back to the apartment building. She stared for a moment at the doors to the building, reluctant to face her empty apartment and the telephone that would force her to pour out her heartrending story to Ben and Murphy.

With a sigh she pulled open the door and walked across the lobby.

"Miss Holland?" a hushed voice called.

"What? Oh, hi, Gus," she said.

"Um, Miss Holland, I think you'd better get him out of here before someone complains."

"Him who?"

"Dr. Shay. He's asleep over there." Gus pointed across the room.

"He's what?" she gasped, spinning around. Taylor lay sprawled in one of the overstuffed chairs and she hurried over to him. "Taylor, wake up," she said, tugging on his sleeve.

"Huh?"

"Wake up. You can't sleep here."

"Blaze?" he said, struggling to his feet.

"Come upstairs, Taylor, before you get arrested for loitering." Why was he here? she thought wildly. Did this mean he wasn't angry anymore?

"I have to talk to you, Blaze," he said, his voice sounding strange to her ears.

"Have you been drinking?" she whispered.

"No. It's just very cold in here. My tongue isn't working right."

Blaze scrutinized Taylor's face. His gray eyes seemed cloudy and his cheeks were unnaturally flushed. She put her hand on his forehead. "My God," she said, "you're burning up with fever."

"I'm not hot, I'm freezing," he mumbled.

Taking him firmly by the arm she led him to the waiting elevator. Taylor leaned his head back against the elevator wall and closed his eyes. His breathing sounded labored and raspy. Once inside her apartment, Blaze planted him on the sofa. "Want some aspirin?" she asked.

"No, I took some but it didn't help."

"You're sick, Taylor. I knew you would be after getting cold and wet last night. This is all my fault and I'm so sorry."

"Blaze, we've got to talk." He took her hands and she could feel the unhealthy heat emanating from his moist skin.

"You need to rest."

"Are you going to listen to me?" he snapped angrily.

"Yes. Okay. Then will you go to bed?"

"Will you come with me?" He smiled, gazing at her with soupy, feverish eyes.

"Do you have amnesia as well as the flu? You're not speaking to me anymore, remember?"

"Blaze, I've gone over last night a thousand times in my mind. I said some terrible things to you and I hope you'll accept my apology. I was just so hurt to think you'd kept something as important as Jeremiah Wade from me. But now I understand that it was your decision, your choice to make, and I had no right to condemn you because you didn't confide in me. I—"

"Oh, Taylor, I should have. It doesn't even make sense to me how I could tell you about my butterflies and still hide Jake Stalker behind a locked door. I was confused, but now I understand myself and I . . . Well, let's just say I'm not muddled anymore."

"Then you forgive me?"

"Only if you forgive me."

"Oh, Blaze, I . . . you mean so much to me. I was miserable last night. I—" Taylor's words were cut short by a severe coughing spell that brought Blaze instantly to her feet.

"You're going to bed right now," she said, dragging him up and peeling off his overcoat.

"Sex maniac."

"To bed alone, Professor. You're very ill, Taylor, and it's not funny." She pulled off her own jacket.

"Heidi. That's who you are today," he said thickly, looking at the ski sweater. "There's the mountain where she lived with that old guy and—"

"Yes, yes, you're right. Move your feet one in front of the other down the hall. Come on, Taylor."

He stood weaving slightly as Blaze threw back the blankets on the bed. She lowered him to a sitting position and unbuttoned his shirt, which was stained with perspiration and sticking to his chest.

After tugging off his shoes and socks she eyed his dark slacks thoughtfully. "Do you think you can get your pants off by yourself?" she asked.

"Sure," he said, flopping back onto the pillow and closing his eyes.

"Then do it!"

"Do what?"

"Take off your pants."

"Too tired," he muttered.

"Oh, brother." She undid the leather belt and, after hesitating a moment, unzipped the slacks and drew them over his long legs, leaving him clad only in his underwear. "This somehow lacks the sparkle of a romantic interlude."

"Huh?"

"Taylor," she said, drawing the blankets up and sitting down next to him, "I'm worried about you. I think I should try to find a doctor who'll make a house call."

"No," he said fiercely. "I'm not that sick. Crawl in here with me, Blaze. Let's finish making up from our awful argument properly. I need to know things are really back to where they were."

But they aren't, Taylor, she thought sadly. Now she knew she loved him and soon he'd be gone again. Only this time he wouldn't be back. "Tell you what," she said. "You get up and do ten push-ups and I'll believe you aren't as sick as I think you are and I'll jump all over your body."

"Oh-h-h-h," he moaned, holding his head. "Push-ups? Are you crazy?"

"I rest my case. Listen, about the doctor, I—"

"All I need is a nap, Blaze. One hour. I'll be fine, you'll see. Could you turn down the heat? It's so damn hot in here."

"I know," she said softly, gently stroking his fevered brow. "You sleep. I'll sit right by the bed."

"That's nice." He smiled. "Now you're Florence Nightingale. I think that's really . . . quite . . . lovely. . . ." His eyes closed and he fell into a deep sleep.

The hour stretched into two as Taylor slept restlessly, pushing away the blankets and the sweat-soaked sheets. Blaze felt a panic rising within her as he began to mumble incoherently, his breathing sounding harsh and constricted in the quiet room. As the perspiration seemed to pour off his body she suddenly remembered she should be replacing his fluids and ran to the kitchen for a glass of water.

"Taylor," she said, shaking him by the shoulder, "wake up just for a minute and have a drink. Taylor? My God, Taylor!"

With trembling hands she shook him violently, calling to him over and over but getting no response. Oh, my God, I can't wake him up, she thought frantically. Oh, Taylor. She stumbled to the telephone and dialed the number of Ben's apartment, praying he was at home.

"Hello."

"Uncle Ben, thank God."

"Blaze, I've been trying to reach you to—"

"Uncle Ben, I need you. It's Taylor. He's sick, really sick. Oh, Uncle Ben, I can't wake him up. He's just lying there and—"

"Where are you?"

"Right here."

"Damn it, Blaze, where?"

"In my apartment and Taylor is—"

"I'm on my way."

Hanging up the phone Blaze sat down beside Taylor, again calling his name and slapping him lightly on the cheek. He moaned once but did not open his eyes. She stared at him, frozen with fear.

Hurry, please, Uncle Ben, she pleaded silently. You've got to help me.

The loud knock at the door sent her racing down the hall, a wave of relief sweeping over her as she pulled Ben inside by the arm. "Oh, Uncle Ben, I'm so glad you're here."

"Where is he?"

"In my bed."

In long, swift strides Ben walked down the hall and into the bedroom. He put a hand on Taylor's forehead. "Hot as hell," he said. "Taylor, come on. Time to wake up," he called, cupping Taylor's face in his hands. "He's out cold, Blaze."

"What does that mean? Why won't he open his eyes?"

"Shhh." Ben dropped to one knee and leaned his head on Taylor's chest. For agonizing moments he listened as Blaze wrung her hands. "Damn," Ben said, getting to his feet. "It sounds like a rushing waterfall in there. I think he's got pneumonia, Blaze. He's a sick man, there's no denying it."

"Oh, no! We've got to get him to a doctor," she said, willing herself not to cry.

"You call an ambulance. I'm going up for my coat and I'll be right back. Move, Blaze. Now!"

Somehow she managed to dial the emergency number and request assistance, carefully giving her address and the apartment number, then she called Gus downstairs.

"Security."

"Gus? This is Blaze Holland."

" 'Evening, Miss Holland. You just caught me. I'm going off duty in about ten minutes. Is there something I can do for you?"

"Gus, listen to me. Dr. Shay is very ill and there's an ambulance on the way. I want you to get the elevator down to the ground floor and hold it there. If anyone tries to take it up, threaten to shoot them."

"Dr. Shay is sick? I thought he was . . . don't you worry, Miss Holland, I'll plant myself by the elevator and it won't move until those medical people get here. Nobody goes up or down until Dr. Shay gets the help he needs."

"Oh, Gus, thank you. Thank you."

"You bet, Miss Holland."

Blaze hung up and hurried back to Taylor's side. His restless tossing and turning had ceased and he lay totally still, his handsome features relaxed, giving the appearance that he was enjoying a peaceful slumber. Blaze picked up his hand and held it against her cheek, and his burning flesh seemed to scorch her.

Oh, Taylor. I love you so much. You've got to be all right. This is all my fault. You came here wet and cold because you were worried about the way I was behaving. I'm sorry. I'm so sorry, Taylor. Open your eyes. Smile at me. Yell at me. Do something! But don't be so still, so quiet. I'll never stop loving you. I know you don't love me because you're stronger than I am and you won't allow yourself to fall into that trap. I understand and I know that loving you means we will be finished. But, Taylor, don't be sick anymore. Please. Wake up and tell me I look like Snow White or Peter Pan or a grape or—

"Blaze?" Ben said softly, coming up behind her. "Did you make the call?"

"Yes, they're on the way. Gus is holding the elevator downstairs."

"Good thinking. Any change here?"

"No, he hasn't moved. It's all my fault, you know."

"Now, Blaze, you can't—"

"It's true. He had to walk here in the rain last night to see why I was so upset after the lecture."

"That was his decision to make."

"I told him I was Jeremiah Wade."

"That's fine, Blaze," he said gently.

"I love him, Uncle Ben. I love Taylor with my whole heart."

"I know that."

"It seems everyone knew before I did. He doesn't love me, though. But I don't care just as long as he gets well," she said, swallowing the lump in her throat.

"We'll get him the best care possible, Blaze. He's young and strong and he'll whip this thing. Honey, does Taylor know you're in love with him?"

"No."

"Did he say he isn't in love with you?"

"No."

"Don't you two talk to each other?" Ben roared, only to frown and glance quickly at the younger man, still lying motionless on the bed.

Blaze sighed. "It's very complicated. "We—"

The telephone rang and Ben rushed to answer it. "Yes?" He listened for a minute, then said, "Thanks for the help, Gus." He hung up the phone and turned to Blaze. "Go to the door," he ordered. "They're on their way."

Again Blaze ran down the hall and flung upon the door, waving frantically as she saw two men step out of the elevator, one bending over as he pulled a collapsed stretcher behind him. "Here," she called, "over here. Are you doctors?"

"Paramedics, ma'am," the one with the stretcher said. "Where's the patient?"

"Down the hall in the bedroom. Oh, please hurry. He's so sick. He's—"

"Yes, ma'am. Everything is under control," he said reassuringly as he hurried past her. Blaze followed the two men and stood watching as they went to

Taylor's side. Ben pulled her close, his arm tightly gripping her shoulders.

"High fever. Real high," one of the men said.

"Let me listen to his chest. You record pulse and B.P.," the other said.

"What's B.P.?" Blaze whispered.

"Blood pressure," Ben said.

"Why don't they just pick him up and haul him to the hospital?" she asked frantically.

"They know what they're doing. Relax."

The first man scribbled something on a pad of paper as the other turned to Blaze. "How old is he? Thirty-five? Thirty-six?"

"Thirty-six."

"Name?"

"Dr. Taylor Shay."

"Okay, jot this down," he said to his partner. "Shay, Taylor, Doctor. Thirty-six, about six-feet-four, two hundred, maybe two ten. Appears to be in excellent shape. Definite fluid in the lungs. First signs of dehydration evident. I'm betting on a roaring case of pneumonia. Let's wrap him up and get him on the stretcher and start an IV. Vitals are not terrific and I get little response to sound or pain. Let's move it."

"My God," Blaze gasped.

"Easy, honey," Ben said. "That was nothing we didn't already know."

"But—"

"Shhh."

With speed and efficiency, the men wrapped Taylor in a blanket and lifted him onto the stretcher. When they set him down, he moaned and opened his eyes half way. "Blaze?" he said weakly.

"Easy does it," one of the paramedics said. "You're going to be fine."

"Damn it," Taylor mumbled. "Where's Blaze?"

Blaze started to go to him, only to be held back by

Ben. "He's calling for me," she said, tears glistening in her eyes.

"You'll only get in their way," Ben said. "Stay put."

"What in the hell have you done with Blaze?" Taylor suddenly roared, sitting up and shoving one of the paramedics with such force that he went sprawling onto his backside.

"Lady," the other man said, backing away from Taylor's menacing glare, "I sure hope you're Blaze."

"Yes, yes, I am. Taylor, I'm here," she said, going quickly to him. "Lie down, please! These men are doctors and they're going to take you to the hospital." She placed her hands on his chest and pushed him back on the stretcher.

"The hell they are!"

"Taylor, you're very sick and . . . Taylor?"

"He's out," the paramedic said, still rubbing the injured area of his anatomy. "Man, I'd hate to have him mad at me when he's feeling good. Let's get that IV going."

"May I ride in the ambulance?" Blaze asked.

"Oh, you'd better believe it." The man grinned. "If he comes around again I sure don't want to be the one to explain to him why you're not there."

"Tell me where you're taking him and I'll follow in a taxi," Ben said. "Blaze, get your coat."

"What?"

"Your coat. One case of pneumonia in this family is enough."

Blaze hurried to the living room and pulled on her down coat, then paused when she noticed Taylor's still damp overcoat lying in a heap on the sofa. She spread it out carefully to dry, then rested her hand on the plush lining and gazed at the coat fondly. A sound behind her caused her to turn and she saw the paramedics rolling the stretcher into the living room.

"Go with them, Blaze," Ben said. "I'll lock up here and be right along."

Nodding, she moved with the solemn procession down the hall and into the waiting elevator. The night security guard who had debated with Taylor over the Giants and the Rams punched the button as they entered and the car immediately began its slow descent.

"I'm sure sorry about this, Miss Holland," the guard said quietly. "Dr. Shay is a good man and . . . they'll fix him up fine, don't you worry."

"Thank you," she said, her gaze never leaving Taylor's flushed face.

In swift, smooth movements they were across the lobby and out the door. The paramedics worked in perfect unison getting the stretcher into the back of the ambulance. Blaze scrambled in with one of the men while the other slid behind the wheel and set the vehicle roaring into action. With lights flashing in the winter night, the siren screaming to clear a path in the traffic, they sped away with their precious cargo.

Blaze stared at Taylor, who was still oblivious to the commotion around him. The paramedic rechecked his pulse. "We'll be there in a jiffy, ma'am," he said. "You'd be surprised how fast you can get across town when you're making this much noise."

"Taylor didn't hurt you, did he? He hit you pretty hard."

"Nothing injured but my pride." The man smiled. "I don't think I'll tell my kids about it, though. Being knocked on my tail by a very sick guy does not a hero make. Say, wasn't that other man Benjamin Kiowa?"

"Yes, he's my uncle."

"No kidding? I have everything he's written. I recognized him from his picture on the book jackets. Had the circumstances been different I would have asked him for his autograph."

"After what you've done for Taylor tonight I'd be more than happy to get Uncle Ben's autograph for you."

"Great. Then I *will* be a hero at home." The man grinned. "I really enjoy all that history about the Indians. And when I want to read about cowboys, I turn to my old buddy Jake Stalker, those books by Jeremiah Wade. Terrific stuff."

"Thank you. I mean, on behalf of my uncle I thank you for the compliment."

"Blaze?" Taylor mumbled.

"Oh, boy," the paramedic muttered. "Nail down the furniture, folks, the slugger is waking up again."

"I'm right here, Taylor, and I won't leave you," Blaze said, leaning close to him.

"Think it's time to stop . . . must tell you . . . I . . ."

"Don't try to talk," she said. "Just rest."

"No!" he said, and fell asleep.

The paramedic chuckled. "Tough dude. Bet he played a little football in his day."

"Michigan State," Blaze said.

"Thought so. That was a sledgehammer that knocked me over. You know, ma'am, I see a lot of horrible things on this run. We get stabbings, wife beatings, child abuse, some really bad stuff. It kind of renews my faith in things to see a couple like you and the doc here. You obviously really care about each other and it's pretty nice to see that."

"I—"

"There's the hospital. Everything is going to be A-okay. You're doing just super, ma'am. Just hang on for a little longer and then, if you're like my wife, you can have yourself a long cry when it's all over."

"I think that's probably on my agenda," she said smiling. "You've been very kind."

"My pleasure, ma'am."

In a blur of activity the ambulance backed into the

emergency entrance, the doors were yanked open, and Taylor was carried away by new faces. Blaze followed quickly, only to see the stretcher disappear behind swinging doors.

"Sorry, dear," a nurse said, "but you can't go in there."

"But—"

"They'll be out to talk to you just as soon as they know something. Why don't you sit down right over here and answer a few questions for me."

With a sigh Blaze sank into a plastic chair, her eyes riveted on the doors that held Taylor captive from her view. Mechanically she answered as best she could the nurse's questions about Taylor, brushing the tears from her cheeks as the icy chill of loneliness swept over her.

Eight

Twenty minutes later Blaze was so tense her jaw ached from clenching her teeth. She stared at the offensive doors, sending them silent messages to open, but they remained closed, a barrier separating her and Taylor. She hated that color, she thought irrationally, staring at the wooden panels. And that tile on the floor was no great shakes either. It smelled funny and all the nurses' shoes squeaked. This place was disgusting. She was going to drag Taylor out of here and take him home. She'd just march in, announce the party was over, and—

"Blaze?"

"What?" she shrieked, jumping to her feet. "Oh, Uncle Ben." She sank back into her chair. "You scared me to death."

"Sorry, honey. Any word?"

"Nothing. They took him in there and no one has come out. I think they're holding him hostage. Maybe they're so dumb they can't figure out what's wrong with him. Oh, no, what if they forgot him? Just dumped him off and—"

"Blaze, stop it. Calm down. It hasn't been that long."

"Approximately twelve years, give or take a century. Oh, Uncle Ben, I'm so worried. What if—"

"Would you just cool it? You look terrible. You're as white as a ghost. Taylor at least had some color in his face. When did you eat last?"

"Eat?"

"Food, Blaze."

"Last night, I guess."

"Damn it," Ben said, and marched off down the hall.

"Well, you don't have to get all in a fuss about it," she muttered.

Ben returned and shoved two candy bars and a bottle of soda into her hands. "Here," he said, "this will perk you up for a little while and I'll get you something more substantial later."

"Thanks. Damn, why don't they come out of there?"

"Look, they have to X-ray his lungs, take blood tests, things like that. It takes time."

"Don't you think this place smells weird?"

"Lord, Blaze, do you have any other complaints? Eat your junk food and shut up for now."

"You don't have to bite my head off."

"I'm sorry, honey," he said, patting her on the knee. "This thing with Taylor has been upsetting."

"You're fond of him, aren't you?"

"Yes, I am. He's a good man, Blaze."

"I know," she said softly, forcing herself to take a bite of the candy. "They made this thing the year of the flood," she said with disgust.

"Just poke it in your mouth and chew," Ben said.

"Boy, whoever picked the paint colors for this place must have had a hangover. This is depressing."

She nodded. "Now you're catching on. God, why doesn't someone tell us how Taylor is?"

"He probably decked them all," Ben said with a soft chuckle.

The minutes dragged by as Blaze finished her snack, the second candy bar proving to be in worse condition than the first, and drank the flat soda. Suddenly the doors swung open and a man dressed in white emerged. He smiled as Blaze and Ben got quickly to their feet.

"Hello," the man said. "If Dr. Shay's rantings and ravings mean anything, you must be Blaze."

"Yes, Blaze Holland, and this is Benjamin Kiowa."

The two men shook hands while Blaze waited anxiously for the man to continue speaking. "I'm Dr. Cole," he said.

"How's Taylor? Please tell me what's going on," Blaze said, feeling the tears threatening once again.

The doctor looked serious as he massaged the back of his neck. "Well, he's got a dandy case of pneumonia. My chief concern at this point, however, is his high temperature. We've started medication and my hope is that the fever will break before morning. We've put him on oxygen to enable him to breathe more comfortably. Right now it's wait and see."

"But—" Blaze started.

"He's young and was in superb physical condition before this hit him," the doctor went on. "Everything is in his favor. Besides that, he's mad as hell and that helps, believe me."

"May I see him?" Blaze asked, her voice hardly above a whisper.

"I don't see why not, except you must understand he won't be aware you're even there. He's doped up pretty good. I was going to put him in Intensive Care, but there's a room on the fourth floor right next to the nurses' station and we can keep a close eye on him there just as well. They're taking him up now. You can sit with him if you like. And, considering what he did to that paramedic, we'll waive visiting hours for you and you can stay as long as you like. But maybe you should go home and get some rest—"

"No, I couldn't leave him."

"Didn't think so." Dr. Cole smiled. "Okay, go on up. It's room four-fourteen. I'll look in on him later. I've left orders for his temperature to be taken every fifteen minutes. That's what we're waiting for, a drop in that fever. After that we'll be on the right road."

"Thank you so much, Dr. Cole," she said.

"Appreciate it," Ben said.

"That's what I'm here for," the doctor said. "I'll see you folks later."

Without speaking Blaze and Ben walked to the elevator. Blaze's heart was beating so wildly she was sure Ben could hear it. They got off on the fourth floor and walked to Taylor's room, and Blaze was surprised to see that her hand was trembling as she tentatively pushed open the door. The glow from a small lamp cast eerie shadows about the room. Taylor's massive frame seemed to fill his bed as he lay motionless in a white hospital gown, an oxygen tent around his upper body and head. A short, plump nurse was smoothing the blankets; then she snapped the rails in place on each side of the narrow bed. An intravenous bottle hung overhead, fluid dripping in a slow, steady rhythm.

"Oh, hello," the nurse said with a smile when Blaze and Ben entered the room. "He's snug as a bug."

"The doctor said I could sit with him," Blaze whispered.

"That's fine," the woman said, "but you don't have

to be so quiet, dear. Dr. Shay can't hear a thing. Make yourself comfortable, I'll be back in a bit."

Blaze moved to Taylor's side, placing her hand gently on his. "Oh, Uncle Ben," she said, unable to stop the tears that spilled from her eyes, "he looks . . . awful."

"That's not very complimentary," Ben said. "Sit down. I'll go find something for you to eat."

"I'm not hungry."

"I don't care. If you intend to stay here all night you'll need your strength or you'll end up a patient yourself."

"I suppose you're right."

"You would have thought they could have gotten him a bigger bed. I'm going to speak to someone about this," Ben said, heading for the door. "The man is sleeping on a postage stamp, for God's sake."

Blaze sank into the chair and stared at Taylor's face. Oh, Taylor, she thought, how did this happen? One minute you were fine and the next . . . If only she could turn back the clock. If only it hadn't rained. If only she hadn't acted like such a child after the lecture. There was so much she was sorry about, but she wasn't sorry she loved him. He was her life, more important to her than Jake or Jeremiah or anyone. Please, Taylor, fight this thing. Stay mad like the doctor said and beat that fever all to hell. Hang on, Taylor—

"Okay, Handsome, let's check your temperature," the plump nurse said, startling Blaze out of her anguished thoughts. The woman placed a thermometer in Taylor's mouth after reaching into the oxygen tent. The slim stick was connected to a small box she held in her hand and Blaze could see blue numbers racing across a screen. "Tsk, tsk," the nurse clucked. "That's not very cooperative, Dr. Shay. We could fry an egg on your head."

"He's no better?" Blaze asked.

"Not yet, dear, but the medication needs time to get into his system. I'll be back in fifteen minutes." She settled the tent back into place.

Ben didn't return and the nurse came bustling in a quarter of an hour later, speaking to Taylor as though he could hear her and scolding him when there was no improvement in his temperature.

"Would you believe," Ben said, when he finally strode into the room, "they don't have any bigger beds? What if Taylor had played basketball instead of football? He'd be hanging off the end of the damn thing. Here." He handed Blaze a sandwich wrapped in cellophane and two small cartons of milk. "Eat this."

"They probably made this for the troops of the Civil War," she said, eyeing the sandwich. "Taylor's temperature is still high, Uncle Ben."

"Give it time. We'd better get organized. I really don't want to leave you here alone, Blaze."

"I'm not alone, I'm with Taylor," she said softly.

"Well said." Ben nodded thoughtfully. "There's really no point in both of us sitting and staring at him. I'll go on home but you call the minute there's any change. I don't care what time it is."

"All right."

"I'll track down some big shot from the university and fill him in. They'll need to know why Taylor's not going to show up for classes tomorrow."

"I never even thought of that."

"Is there anyone else who should be notified, Blaze?"

"Clare and Bill. They'd be terribly upset to think Taylor was ill and they didn't know."

"Will you handle that?"

"Yes, and I'll call Murphy in the morning."

"Okay, we're all set. Remember, call me."

"I will. Uncle Ben, thank you so much for everything. I don't know what I would have done without you."

"You would have gotten him here on your own. You're a lot tougher than you give yourself credit for. Good night, honey, try to catch a nap."

"Good night, Uncle Ben."

Blaze decided not to call Clare and Bill until the nurse had checked Taylor's temperature again, hoping to have better news to share with the Scotts. She ate the sandwich, which was dry and tasteless, and washed it down with the milk, which was warm. When the nurse merely frowned and shook her head upon her next visit, Blaze sighed and left the room in search of a telephone book.

The directory listed twenty-two William Scotts and she couldn't remember the name of the street Bill and Clare lived on. After Blaze had dialed the wrong William Scott four times, Clare's familiar voice at last came on the line.

"Clare? It's Blaze Holland."

"Blaze, my goodness, what a surprise."

"Not a happy one, I'm afraid. Taylor's sick. He has pneumonia, Clare, and he's in the hospital. I'm here with him."

"My God, how serious is it?"

"His fever is very high. The doctor's concerned about that. I'm not leaving until I know the crisis has passed."

"Damn it," Clare said. "I can't even get there. Bill is out of town and I'll never find a sitter this late."

"Don't worry. He wouldn't even know it if you were here. I'll call you as soon as there's news." Blaze gave Clare all the necessary details: hospital name and address, phone and room numbers. Her voice was unnaturally low and quavery.

"Oh, Blaze, this is frightening."

"I know."

"I'm so glad you're with him. He'd be happy if he knew. I'll come in the morning but do call me in the meantime if—"

"I will. Good night, Clare."

"Thank you, Blaze. Thank you so much."

The passing of time was recorded by the coming and going of the nurse who smiled at Blaze and carried on her one-sided conversation with Taylor. As it neared eleven o'clock Blaze was stiff from sitting in the chair and took to pacing the room to loosen up her muscles. Taylor's raging fever wasn't breaking.

"Here I am again," the nurse said cheerfully, bouncing into the room once more. "You really should try to rest, dear. Why don't you curl up on that other bed?"

"I might later, but not yet. Shouldn't his temperature be lower by now? You said the medication would—"

"Well, let us just find out. Dr. Shay, you've got this pretty little woman all upset about you. It's time to start behaving yourself." The nurse placed the thermometer in Taylor's mouth. "Oh, bless his heart."

"What is it?" Blaze asked anxiously.

"Down three degrees. That's my boy," she said, readjusting the oxygen tent. "I'll go put in a call to the doctor. Now we're getting somewhere. About time too, Dr. Shay. You've given us all enough of a scare. Shame on you. And you, dear, get some sleep."

"Yes, ma'am," Blaze found herself saying under the nurse's stern look.

In the quiet room Blaze lifted Taylor's hand to her cheek. He did feel cooler, and tears of relief and fatigue clouded her vision. Dr. Cole arrived and nodded his approval at his patient's progress. Blaze called Ben and Clare with the news that Taylor's fever had broken and was dropping rapidly, hovering now just above normal. Both were delighted and promised to visit the next day. After she had hung up, Blaze kissed Taylor on the forehead, crawled into the other bed, pulled a spare blanket over her and fell instantly asleep.

Some small sound startled Blaze from her sleep, and she sat up abruptly, not sure where she was. She rubbed her eyes, then it all came back to her, and she looked over at Taylor. The oxygen tent was gone and Taylor seemed to be in a natural sleep, rather than unconscious.

She went into the small bathroom and splashed cold water on her face, then took a comb from her purse and ran it through her thick hair. She had just settled in the rock hard chair when Taylor stirred, moaned softly, and opened his eyes. "Blaze?" he said, his voice faint.

"I'm here, Taylor," she said, leaning over the railing on the bed.

"Did you redecorate? I liked how you had it before. The bed's shrunk too."

"You're not in my bedroom, you're at the hospital."

"Am I having a baby?" he asked, a crooked smile on his face.

"You had twins. You're a medical marvel."

"Good for me. God, there's a brick on my chest. What in the hell is going on?"

"You have pneumonia, Taylor, but you're going to be fine."

"What time is it?"

"I don't know. Early morning."

"What happened to last night?"

"You missed it. Too bad, because it was a barrel of laughs."

"You still look like Heidi. Have you been here all this time?"

"Yes."

"For me?"

"For you, Taylor," she said, her voice whisper soft.

"God, Blaze, I . . . what a mess. I'm sorry for causing all this trouble. Hell, I've got to get to work."

"Uncle Ben called the university and told them you're ill. Taylor, calm down. You've got to rest."

"Rest?"

"Rest."

He fell back, asleep.

When Taylor woke again several hours later, he wasn't as tractable.

"What's this junk?" he asked, looking at the IV equipment.

"Haven't you ever been in a hospital before?"

"No, and I'm not staying in this one," he declared, his voice rising.

"What's all the yelling about?" Clare said, startling them both as she suddenly entered the room. "Lord, Taylor, I heard you halfway down the hall. For a sick man you sure are noisy. Hi, Blaze, how's the trouble-maker here?"

"I'm getting out of this dump, Clare," Taylor growled.

"Oh, really?" Clare glared at the IV. "Appears to me you're wired for sound. I'd say you're a captive audience."

"Where are my clothes?" he asked.

"On the floor in my bedroom," Blaze said, folding her arms across her breasts. "You're stuck, Shay, so relax and enjoy it."

"Like hell!"

"Good morning," a pleasant voice sang out as a mammoth woman in a nurse's uniform pushed a cart into the room. "My, aren't we wide awake? And how are we feeling?"

"I don't know about you," Taylor said, glaring at the nurse, "but I feel like—"

"Taylor, watch your mouth," Blaze interrupted.

"If you ladies will excuse us," the nurse said, "it's time for our bath."

"What?" Taylor yelled.

"Of course," Clare said, taking Blaze by the arm. "We'll go have a cup of coffee."

"Now wait just a damn minute." Taylor raised his hand in protest. "Nobody's giving me a bath!"

"And a shave," the nurse added.

"Oh, no, you don't!" he said, shaking his head. "You just keep your hands off me, lady."

"Come on, Blaze," Clare said grinning. "He'll be well taken care of."

"Blaze! Clare! Don't you leave me alone with . . . her!" Taylor hollered, his voice following them down the hall.

"Oh, dear," Blaze said.

"I love it," Clare chortled. "I'd say he's making a splendid recovery."

In a few minutes the two women were seated in the cafeteria sipping cups of strong coffee. Clare stirred the liquid slowly as if deep in thought. "Blaze," she finally said, "your staying with Taylor was really wonderful. I know he's acting like a bear right now, but it must have been a hideous night before his fever broke."

"He was so still, so quiet. The yelling he's doing is like music to my ears," Blaze said softly.

"You're in love with him, aren't you?"

"I . . ."

"Please, Blaze, it's important to me that I know."

Blaze sighed. "Yes, Clare, I'm in love with Taylor. But you must promise me you won't say a word to him about it because I don't want to leave him until he's really well again."

"I don't understand."

"Clare, Taylor is not now, nor will he ever be, in love with me. We made an agreement and the fact that I lost control of my feelings for him will mean the end of our relationship."

"But that's crazy!"

"It's the way it is. I want to know he's all right before it's over. Please, Clare, promise me you won't tell him."

"Blaze, you're making a mistake. Taylor is—Oh, damn it, he's got me caught right in the middle of this."

"Promise me, Clare."

"Yes. Yes, I promise but—"

"Thank you."

"I suppose we'd better go back and see who won the war."

"Did you see the size of that woman?" Blaze laughed. "Taylor didn't stand a chance."

"Serves him right. Sick or not, I'd like to strangle him."

"Why?"

"Someday I'll be able to tell you. I hope."

"You're confusing me, Clare."

"If I'm not making sense it's because Taylor Shay has driven me insane. Let's go."

The expression on Taylor's face when they returned to his room was stormy. The IV had been removed and he was sitting up against the pillows, a tray with a bowl of jello and a cup of tea in front of him. He was clean shaven and had on a pale blue gown. "Thanks for nothing," he said, staring at the green jello.

"Are we all squeaky clean?" Clare asked.

"I'm warning you, Clare."

"Oh, hush, Taylor. You're not the first person in the

world to ever have a sponge bath," she said. "You scared the hell out of everyone last night and poor Blaze was all alone and—"

"I know," he said, looking at Blaze. "I'm sorry."

"That's better," Clare said. "Eat your jello."

"I hate jello."

"That does it!" Clare smacked him on the foot. "I'm going to go get that Amazon and have her feed you."

"No! Wait! I'll eat it. See? I'm taking a bite. Great stuff. Delicious."

"Ignore him, Blaze," Clare said. "He's ridiculous. You should go home and get some sleep. Taylor, tell her to go home."

"Blaze, I'll take you to your apartment now," he said.

Blaze laughed. "Nice try. I'll go as soon as the doctor has been around."

"Who's using my name in vain?" a man said, coming into the room. Perhaps sixty, he had a thinning crop of gray hair and a warm smile. "I'm Dr. Wood. I'm in charge of you during the day because I'm old and I refuse to work nights. Ugh. How can you eat that slimy stuff? I can't stand jello."

"Don't have a pizza on you, do you?" Taylor asked, scowling again.

"I'll see what I can do. Let's have a look here." Dr. Wood flipped through Taylor's chart. "Whew! You gave them a run for their money, didn't you? Typical pneumonia case. One minute at death's door and then the fever breaks and you're all rise and shine. How are you feeling?"

"Fine."

"No you're not. Your chest hurts, you're tired and weak, and you have a headache."

"Well, other than that I feel fine."

"And I suppose you want to get the hell out of this place?" The doctor smiled.

"You've got it, doc."

The doctor swung back the hospital tray and stood by the side of the bed looking down at Taylor. "Well, what we're looking at here is bed rest for a good week or so. There's no magic drug I can give you. Viral pneumonia has to run its course. We're pumping antibiotics into you, but that's to prevent a secondary bacterial infection. Now, according to the information in your chart you're not married and unless there's someone who can fix your meals and—"

"He lives with me," Blaze said. Did I say that? she thought, shaking her head slightly.

"I do? I mean, I do," Taylor said, looking at Blaze with wide eyes.

"You know how it is with these modern relationships," Clare added. "Blaze will take excellent care of him."

"Well . . ." The doctor stroked his chin thoughtfully. "I'll tell you what. Stay put for twenty-four hours to make sure that fever doesn't spike again and if it doesn't, I'll discharge you tomorrow morning. That is with the understanding that you stay in bed and come see me in a week."

"I love to stay in bed," Taylor said, grinning at Blaze, who blushed a lovely pink.

"You're having delusions of grandeur, hot shot," the older man cackled. "You're weak as a kitten and definitely out of commission. Well, enjoy your jello. I'll look in on you later."

"Don't forget the pizza," Taylor called after him.

"Okay, Blaze, I'm going home to my brood," Clare said, "and you're leaving and getting some rest. Kiss Ugly good-bye."

"God, you're bossy," Taylor said. "Ten minutes. Give me ten minutes with Blaze."

"Okay, but that's it. The poor girl is exhausted and you should take a nap yourself. 'Bye, love." Clare leaned over and kissed him on the cheek. "Oh, you smell so nice after your little bath."

"You tell Bill about that, I'll never speak to you again, Clare."

She laughed. "Cross my palm with silver."

"Thanks for coming, Clare," Taylor said, his voice sincere.

"Please do as the doctors say," she said quietly. "You're very important to a lot of people, Taylor."

"I will."

After Clare had left the room, Taylor turned to Blaze. "Do you realize what you've done?" he asked.

"Me?"

"You told that doctor that I live with you and you'd take care of me."

"Well, you said I was Florence Nightingale. I'm just trying to live up to my reputation."

"Be serious. I can't recuperate at your place."

"You don't want to?"

"Hey, it'd be great. Wonderful. But what about Ben?"

"He doesn't live there."

"Would you stop it? Ben will go on the warpath if I move in there."

"Warpath? Is that an ethnic joke?"

"Blaze, take pity on me. I'm a sick man. I'm trying to avoid any trouble for you."

"Taylor, Uncle Ben will understand. Do you know he came down here last night? He was very concerned and he wouldn't want you to be alone until you're on your feet again."

"I'm not sure I'd feel right about you waiting on me hand and foot."

"Taylor, I'm tired and I don't want to hash this over for an hour. Make up your mind. Either you come home with me or stay here. Or, I suppose, you could go to your place and hire someone to come in. Think about it and let me know."

"I want to be with you, Blaze, more than you can imagine. If you're sure it's all right, then that's what I'll do."

"Fine."

"God." He flopped back against the pillows. "I feel faint."

"Oh, no," she gasped. "Can I help?"

"Yes," he said, his voice sounding weak.

"Tell me what to do!"

"Kiss me."

"What? Oh, you fink. You scared me out of my mind."

"Come here," he said softly, holding out his arms. "I need to hold you."

"I'm not sure this is good for you," she said, moving into his embrace.

"Just what the doctor ordered," he murmured, and kissed her deeply. The heat of desire spread through her like a rampant fire.

"I'll see you this afternoon," she said against his lips.

"Thank you for last night, Blaze."

" 'Bye, Taylor." She smiled warmly and wiggled out of his arms. "Eat your jello."

After arriving at her apartment Blaze yawned continually as she scrambled some eggs and consumed them with five slices of toast. She was halfway to the bedroom when the telephone rang.

"Blaze? Murphy. God, I've been a wreck. I was so worried about your reaction to Taylor's lecture and I couldn't find you. I was afraid you'd shot him, rolled him in a ditch, and left town. I got so frantic I called Ben and he told me about Taylor getting sick. How's he doing? And how are you holding up?"

"Boy, Murphy, when you get going . . . Anyway,

Taylor is going to be fine. He just has to rest. I'm okay, only tired. Murphy . . . um . . . I told Taylor that I'm Jeremiah Wade."

"You did? Well, I'm sure he'll respect your secret. That must have been a real wingding of a fight after his speech."

"You could definitely say that, but everything's all right now. I'm bringing him here from the hospital tomorrow to recuperate."

"I was going to come in, but would you prefer I didn't?"

"He's got to stay in bed. There's no reason why we can't work down the hall. It shouldn't disturb him. Why don't you let yourself in with your key in the morning while I'm picking him up?"

"Sounds good. I'll start a batch of my homemade veggie soup when I get there. That'll fix old Taylor right up."

"Thanks, Murphy, you're super."

After hanging up, Blaze called Ben. In a rush of words she explained the plan to bring Taylor to her apartment the next morning, stressing that the doctor had insisted Taylor have total bed rest.

"I see," Ben said as Blaze held her breath. "Seems like a sensible solution."

Thank goodness. Cancel the warpath, she thought. "I'm off for a bath and nap, Uncle Ben," she said cheerfully.

"Okay, talk to you later."

The warm bath water was her final undoing and after slipping on the butterfly nightie, she crawled into bed and fell asleep seconds after her head hit the pillow.

Taylor was sleeping when she arrived at the hospital that evening. As she sat in the familiar chair and gazed at him, her heart seemed to be bursting with love, even as a wave of misery rushed over her.

Tomorrow she would take him home with her, close the door on the world, and nurse him back to health. But when he was strong again he'd look into her eyes and see how much she loved him. Then the door would reopen and he'd walk out and she'd have only the memories left. What had Tilly said? If she fell in love she'd be a better woman for having experienced it? She wasn't sure that was true. She'd be sad and lonely and empty when Taylor was gone. Oh, God, she loved him so much.

"Okay, everybody up," a voice boomed.

"Oh, Dr. Wood," Blaze said as the white-jacketed man entered the room. Taylor stirred and opened his eyes.

"Wake up, Dr. Shay," Dr. Wood said. "I've been by three times and you've slept the day away. That's fine, but now we have important business to attend to."

"If you say I have to submit to another bath I'll—"

"No, no. Sit tight, I'll be right back." Dr. Wood rushed from the room.

Taylor pushed himself up. "Hi, Blaze," he said, smiling.

"Here we go," Dr. Wood called, reappearing with a large white box in his hands. "Pizza!"

"Hey, that's great," Taylor said.

"We should have a cold beer with this," the doctor continued, handing the box to Blaze, "but they'd kick me out of here, so we'll settle for these." He pulled several bottles of soda out of the deep pockets of his white jacket. "Okay, children, let's dig in."

It was like a party. Dr. Wood entertained them with stories about his escapades as a young intern. Blaze looked at Taylor often, relishing his smile, his deep chuckle. After the pizza and soda were all gone and the doctor had sailed from the room, Blaze cleaned up the remains of the meal. By the time she was through, Taylor was sound asleep again. She gently kissed him good night and left.

It had been a strange evening, she thought as she walked outside and took a deep breath of the cold winter air. Sharing a pizza with a friendly old doctor and Taylor propped up in bed, wearing a baggy hospital gown was a little out of the ordinary. She knew he'd be furious when he woke and found he'd fallen asleep without having seen her alone, but it didn't matter because tomorrow she would take him home. Home for a little while anyway.

Nine

The next morning Clare telephoned Blaze to tell her that, since she had a key to Taylor's Pink Palace, as she referred to it, she would stop by and pack some of his things and meet Blaze at the hospital.

"Be sure and bring his razor," Blaze said, "or he'll throw a tantrum."

"I wouldn't trade places with you for anything," Clare said. "He's going to be a rotten patient."

"I'll buy him some new crayons and a coloring book. That'll keep him busy."

Taylor was fuming when Blaze arrived at the hospital. "She did it to me again," he roared. "She gave me a bath in a bucket! Keep that woman away from me or I'll—"

"Now, now," Blaze said, trying not to giggle. "I'm going to take you home and tuck you in bed. I've made you six different flavors of jello."

"Tell me you're joking."

"I'm joking. Actually, Murphy is fixing you some of her famous vegetable soup."

"Blaze," he said softly, taking her hand, "I hardly know what to say about all you've done for me. I—"

"Taylor Shay," Clare yelled, coming into the room carrying a suitcase and a shopping bag, "I searched that Godawful bedroom of yours from top to bottom and I couldn't find your pajamas."

He grinned. "I don't own any."

"Figure you to be decadent. Here." She threw the bag at him. "I went out and bought you a pair. They have little horsies on them."

"No kidding? Aw, shucks, Clare, they're just plain blue." He riffled through his suitcase. "Well, if you ladies will clear out of here, I'll get dressed."

"Taylor," Clare said, planting her hands on her hips, "I have a husband and three sons, so I'm sure you have no surprises in store for me. You're weak and you might need some help."

"Out!" He pointed to the door.

"Come on, Blaze," Clare said, "let's leave Mr. Modest Macho to do his thing. Serve you right if you fall over on your face, Taylor."

Clare shook her head, rolled her eyes, and tapped her foot impatiently out in the hall while Blaze tried desperately not to laugh out loud.

"Okay," Taylor finally called.

"Wonderful," Clare muttered, pushing open the door.

Dressed in jeans and a black V-neck sweater Taylor sat perched on the edge of the bed. "Are you all right?" Blaze asked.

"I feel like I just ran twenty miles," he said, wiping the perspiration from his brow.

"Hello, hello," the large nurse said, pushing a wheelchair into the room.

"Oh, no," Taylor moaned. "Blaze, protect me. She's after me again."

"Come now, Dr. Shay," the woman said with a smile, "hop right in here and I'll give you a ride all the way to the front door."

"And out of your clutches forever," he said under his breath.

"Pardon me?" the nurse asked.

"I just wanted to say," Taylor said, walking to the woman and taking one of her hands in both of his, "how much I appreciate everything you've done to speed my recovery. You are an asset to this fine establishment and you've made my stay here totally . . . enjoyable."

"Oh, my," the nurse said, blushing crimson red. "Aren't you just the sweetest thing?"

"Ever consider going into politics?" Clare whispered in his ear. "You're as phony as a three dollar bill."

Clare drove them to Blaze's apartment but said she couldn't stay.

"Thanks for the pajamas," Taylor said as Clare kissed him good-bye. "I guess."

"I'll call you later, Blaze," Clare said. "If you tell me you've already thrown him out on the sidewalk I'll certainly understand."

Carrying his suitcase in one hand, Blaze helped Taylor into the lobby, where a smiling Gus greeted them.

"Dr. Shay, good to see you," Gus said. "How are you feeling?"

"Okay. Childbirth isn't so tough."

Gus laughed. "That's what I told my wife seven times."

The apartment greeted them with the delicious aroma of Murphy's soup. Blaze propelled Taylor down the hall to the bedroom after he had waved weakly to

Murphy. The bed had already been turned down and Taylor looked at it appreciatively before flopping onto it on his stomach.

"Oh, no you don't," Blaze said. "Get your pajamas on first."

"I can't sleep in those things," he mumbled into the pillow.

"Well, you're not walking around here nude. This is a classy place. Take off your clothes, put on your jammies, and I'll be back in a minute."

"Aren't you going to help me?" he asked, pushing himself up to the edge of the bed.

"You got them on alone, you get them off alone."

"You are not kind." He pulled his sweater over his head. "Tell you what. We'll compromise."

"Oh?"

"I'll wear half of the pajamas. What shall it be? The tops or the bottoms?"

"Are you serious?"

"Yeah."

"Well, then wear the bottoms, for heaven's sake."

"Okay, and you can have the tops when our butterfly's in the wash."

"You've got a deal. But get in bed right now," she commanded as she left the room.

"He looks a little gray around the edges," Murphy said as Blaze walked into the workroom.

"I know. He's awfully weak. I'm going to stay in here for a few minutes and I'll bet he's asleep when I go back."

He was. Dead to the world, and Blaze stared at him for several minutes. He had pulled the blankets up to his waist and she resisted the urge to run her fingertips over his broad, bare chest. Quietly she unpacked his suitcase, placing his belongings securely among her own, and then walked slowly back to the workroom.

"Is he sleeping?" Murphy asked.

"Like a baby. I imagine he will for a couple of hours. Just making the effort to get here really wore him out." Blaze hesitated. "Murphy, I realize now that I'm in love with Taylor, so once he's well our relationship will be over."

"Oh, Blaze."

"But for now he's here and that's what's important. In the meantime, we have a real problem."

"Let me guess. Jake Stalker and the invisible rifle."

"Yes. Oh, Murphy, Taylor was right about everything he said about Jeremiah Wade. I was careless and—"

"But, Blaze, it was only one mistake in so many—"

"That doesn't change the fact that I was wrong," Blaze said adamantly. "I'm so afraid there are errors in both the manuscripts that are at the publisher's now. Murphy, would you please get on the phone and find out when we can see the galleys for book nine? Neither that nor book ten are going to press until I've double-checked everything."

"Do you realize how much time that will take?"

"I don't care. I'm not writing another word on this new one until I'm sure that stuff the editor has is perfect. Please call him, Murphy, and tell him I need it as soon as possible."

"All right, Blaze." Murphy called on the phone in the living room and was back in a few minutes. "You're in luck," she said. "The corrected and revised galleys are back from the printer. Your editor agrees to a last double-double check and I can pick up the galleys this afternoon."

"Great, and then I'm going over every word. I'm not going to ask you to help me. The responsibility is mine. You can type what I've done on the new book, but then it goes on hold."

"That won't keep me busy for long."

"You can cook nifty things for Taylor. I'll kill him off if I do it. Beyond eggs and hamburgers, I'm hopeless."

"Oh, good. I'll whip up some great concoctions. This'll be fun."

When Taylor woke from his nap Blaze brought him a tray with a bowl of Murphy's soup, several slices of toast, and a huge glass of milk. She refilled the bowl three times before he finally said he was full. "Thank you," he said as she sat the tray on the floor. "That was great."

"Do you want to sleep some more?"

"No, I feel pretty good. I think I'm bored already."

Blaze sat down beside him on the bed. "Taylor, can I talk to you?"

"Sure, babe, fire away."

"Murphy has gone to my publisher's to get the galleys for my next Jake Stalker book. I'm going over every detail, Taylor, to make sure I haven't made any—"

"Oh, Blaze," he interrupted. "I'm so sorry about what I said about Jeremiah Wade. If I'd only known that you were—"

"No! You did the right thing. There's no excuse for Jake shooting that rifle. I'm just petrified that there might be inaccurate facts in this next one and I'm going to double check."

"Aren't you on a deadline? That will really slow you down."

"I'll manage somehow."

"Wait a minute," he said thoughtfully. "I have a better idea. I'll proof the galleys."

"You?"

"How can I say this without sounding like a conceited slob? Blaze, I've been studying, reading, and teaching history for years. I know that stuff inside out and what I don't have stored in my head, I can find in reference material that's bibliographed in my brain."

She smiled. "You sound like a conceited slob."

"What can I say? I'm terrific. But seriously, it's true. I caught that bit on the rifle right away."

"You mean you read it and just knew?"

"Yep. It nearly jumped off the page at me. So, don't you see? I can check the book much quicker than you can."

"You'd be willing to do that?" she asked softly.

"I'm going to get cabin fever stuck in this bed and it'll help pass the time. Besides, Blaze, I want that book perfect too. At my next lecture I'll tell everyone that Jeremiah Wade is one of the finest authors in this country, which he . . . you are."

"Thank you, Taylor."

"Come over here, Blaze. If you don't kiss me pretty soon I'm going to have to retrain my lips."

"Is there anything else you'll forget how to do?" she asked, snuggling next to him.

"I don't think we should run that risk, so tonight we'll—"

"Taylor, you heard what the doctor said."

"What does he know? I'm not dead, I'm just a little under the weather."

"We'll see." She laughed softly, running her hand across his chest and down to the waistband of his pajamas, which rested low on his hips.

"Mmmm," he murmured, kissing her neck. "Keep that up and you're going to find out right now just how wrong that doctor was."

"I hear Murphy coming back," Blaze said, kissing him quickly and sliding off the bed. "We're in here, Murphy," she called. "Do you have the galleys?"

"Sure do," Murphy said, coming into the bedroom. "Hi, Taylor."

"Murphy, you make terrific soup," he said.

"I'm glad you enjoyed it. Here are the galleys, Blaze." She held up a large manila envelope. "The editor wants them back in a week, but I told him we'd take as long as we need."

"Give them here," Taylor said. "I'll get started."

"You?" Murphy said, handing him the envelope.

"Taylor's going to check them for accuracy, Murphy," Blaze said.

"That's perfect!" Murphy said. "You have as a resident roommate one of the foremost authorities on this country's history and it never crossed my mind to have him . . . yes, indeed, it's a great idea."

"But"—Blaze looked stern—"Taylor, you must agree that the minute you feel tired you'll rest."

"I don't have much choice in the matter because I keep falling asleep. There's no way I can overdo it. My body just conks out on me. Now, you two go do something constructive and earn your keep. I have work to do."

For the remainder of the afternoon the apartment was quiet except for the sound of the typewriter. Blaze and Murphy worked on Jake Stalker number eleven while Taylor read number nine. Blaze interrupted him several times to see if he wanted anything to eat or drink, but he waved her away absently, obviously deep engrossed in his task.

"Blaze!" he shouted, just before five o'clock.

"Oh, no," she said to Murphy. "He's found a mistake."

She ran down the hall. "Yes?" she said breathlessly.

"Get on the phone!"

"What for?"

"I want to order a covered wagon. We'll set it up right in the living room and—"

"Good-bye, Taylor." She marched from the room.

Murphy put a broccoli and cheese casserole in the oven before leaving for the day. When it was ready Blaze carried two plates of it and two glasses of iced tea into the bedroom. "Thought I would join you for dinner," she said cheerfully. "Hello?"

"What? Oh, hi there. I was really into this. It's an intriguing story and brilliantly written. And, Jeremiah, so far not one fact is off the mark."

"Thank goodness. Let's eat this while it's hot."

They sat propped up against the pillows while they ate, Taylor chatting about scenes in the book that he had particularly enjoyed. "I've always liked Jake," he said. "The arrogant son of a gun."

Blaze laughed. "He is, isn't he? But he sure gets his share of women."

"Let him have them," he said, pulling her close. "I've got the one I want right here."

"Taylor, the dishes!" She set them on the floor then crawled back beside him. "You were saying?"

"Jake and I like action, not words, ma'am," he drawled, and then covered her mouth with his in a deep, passionate kiss that left her weak and breathless.

What a dopey doctor, she thought dreamily, much much later. There was nothing wrong with Taylor Shay. He had fallen asleep soon after their exquisite lovemaking and she had put in a few more hours of work. Now she snuggled contentedly against Taylor's warm muscular body and drifted easily into sleep.

The next morning after breakfast Taylor managed a quick shower and then resumed his work on the galleys. Clare telephoned and Blaze assured her the patient was fine and presently solving a dot-to-dot puzzle. Ben was delighted to hear that Taylor was proofing Blaze's work and told her he would check on them all later. Taylor fell asleep soon after lunch and in the middle of the afternoon, while he was still snoozing, the intercom buzzed.

"Mr. Smith to see you, Miss Holland," Gus said.

Oh, no, it's Brian! she thought frantically. He

couldn't come up here! But it would be really rotten to break it off over an intercom. Taylor was asleep so . . .

"Miss Holland?"

"All right, Gus, send him up."

"Boring Brian is on his way?" Murphy asked, coming out of the workroom.

"What else can I do? I have to tell him in a nice way that I don't want to see him anymore."

"How do you explain the man in your bed?"

"He'll never know. Taylor is sound asleep and I'll tell Brian it's been fun but it's over. Short and sweet."

"I'm getting out of here," Murphy said, retreating into the workroom and shutting the door.

"Brian. My, my. Long time no see," Blaze said as she opened the door. Brian was dressed in a conservative business suit, every strand of his short blond hair in place.

"Blaze." He smiled, took her by the shoulders, and kissed her on the lips. "I missed you."

"How was your trip?"

"Exciting! I can hardly wait to tell you about it. I have information on some new tax shelters that are simply wonderful."

Boring. He really was boring, she thought. She had to get this over with. "Um, Brian, a lot has happened since you went away."

"Oh?"

"You see, I met . . . It's not as though you and I were really serious about each other or anything and . . ."

"What are you saying? I love you, Blaze," Brian said, a little loudly.

"Shh, Murphy is napping. Brian, look, I'm sorry if this will hurt you in any way because I value your friendship, but I have to tell you that—"

"Blaze? Oh, excuse me, I didn't know you had company," Taylor said as he came into the room wearing only his low slung pajama bottoms.

"Taylor! Go back to bed!" she yelled.

"Who in the hell is this?" Brian said.

"Just want some orange juice," Taylor said calmly, walking between the pair and into the kitchen.

"Why is there an undressed man roaming through your apartment, Blaze?" Brian asked, his face flushed with anger.

"He's dressed. Sort of," she said weakly.

"I'm not being much of a host," Taylor said, coming back into the room. "Would you like some juice? By the way, I'm Taylor Shay. Dr. Shay, actually. I'm a brain surgeon."

"No, he's not, Brian. He's a professor," Blaze said.

"And that makes it all right?" Brian said. "What's going on here?"

"Going on?" Taylor raised his eyebrows questioningly, all innocence.

"Taylor, please. Brian, I was trying to explain that since you left town I—"

"Started living with him?" Brian said, gesturing toward Taylor who was busily studying the contents of his glass.

"Not exactly. Taylor is just staying here for a while until—"

"Blaze, you shock me," Brian said stiffly. "I never thought you were the kind of girl who would—"

"Really, old man," Taylor said, a pleasant smile on his face, "where else would you expect me to live except with my beloved . . . wife?"

"Your what?" Blaze and Brian said in unison.

"Blaze and I had hoped to keep it a secret until we took our honeymoon, but I guess the cat's out of the bag." Taylor put his arm around Blaze's shoulders while she stared at him with her mouth open.

"You're married?" Brian croaked.

"Yes," Murphy sang out as she rushed into the gathering. "Isn't it just the sweetest thing? Well,

Brian, express your best wishes and I'll see you to the door. I'll be leaving myself because this dear couple wants to be alone."

"But, Blaze," Brian said, "what about those annuities you wanted to buy and—"

"We'll be in touch," Taylor said, pumping Brian's hand.

Murphy leaned against the door after ushering a sputtering Brian out. "Don't say a word, Blaze, until I'm out of earshot," she said, grabbing her coat and purse. "My nervous system can't take it." The door closed quickly behind her.

"I think I'll take a nap," Taylor said, setting his glass on the end table and walking across the room.

"Taylor, you move and I'll break your kneecaps," Blaze shrieked. "Have you lost your mind? Yes, that's it. The fever fried your brain and you're crazy. Do you know what you've done?"

"Me?"

"Oh, you're impossible. Boring Brian will tell the whole world that you and I are—"

"Is that what you call him? Boring Brian? That's rich. I love it." Taylor laughed uproariously.

"Shut up!"

"Gosh, Blaze, you sure are upset. I was just trying to get you out of an embarrassing situation. I thought it was a pretty good explanation for why I'm here dressed in my finery."

"And how do I explain it when you're no longer on the premises?"

"I hadn't thought of that." He shrugged, turned, and walked down the hall.

"You just stay in there, Taylor Shay," she yelled after him. "Don't come out and don't speak to me. You make me so furious I want to just—"

"Could you keep it down?" he said, poking his head

out of the bedroom. "I'm trying to get some work done around here."

Blaze didn't hear Taylor's deep, throaty chuckle nor see the wide grin on his face as she stomped into the workroom and slammed the door. An hour later he knocked on the door. "Blaze? We had better call a truce for now. There's a problem with the manuscript."

"Really?" she said, flinging the door open. "What's wrong?"

"May I come in?"

"Of course. Sit down. I made a mistake? Oh, Taylor, tell me I didn't."

He nodded. "I'm afraid so. Look at this. You've got Jake unable to read the expression in the outlaw's eyes because of the shadows cast by the bad guy's Stetson."

"Yes, that's right."

"No, that's wrong. Jake is wandering around in this story in 1861. John Batterson Stetson produced the first Stetson hat in Philadelphia in 1865."

"Are you sure?" she whispered.

"Positive. But check it out for yourself." He surveyed her volumes of reference material and handed her a book.

Blaze quickly thumbed through the pages, then groaned when she read about the Stetson. Hot tears sprang to her eyes and she ran down the hall and flung herself across her bed. Taylor followed slowly, shaking his head and frowning. He stretched out next to her and gently rubbed her back. "Hey, come on, don't cry," he said softly. "You know tears get me all shook up. Blaze, I read the entire thing and that's the only mistake. All you have to do is take out the word Stetson and just say he wore a cowboy hat or something."

"That's beside the point," she sniffled, not looking

at him. "I blew it again. I don't deserve to be published anymore. I—"

"Now, just knock it off. You're a good writer and you know it. Jake Stalker will go on for years and years. Besides, you've got your own personal fact checking proofreader right here. You've got it made, Jeremiah."

"Oh, sure," she said, sitting up and facing him. "And after you're gone? Who bails me out then?" She wiped the tears off her cheeks.

"Gone where? You mean in June when the semester is over? I haven't had a chance to tell you, Blaze, but NYU has offered me a contract and—"

"No! I'm not talking about June." She slid off the bed. "It's next week when you're well and I have to tell you . . . tell you . . . Oh, damn it!" she covered her face with her hands as the tears started again.

"Tell me what?" he said, going to her and pulling her hands free.

"That we're finished. Over. Done."

"What are you saying?" A muscle twitched in his jaw.

"I broke the rules, Taylor," she said, her entire body trembling. "I couldn't help it and I've ruined everything. I didn't want you to know until you were better, but it's too late. I can't hide it anymore. I . . . love you, Taylor. I love you so much and I'm sorry. I just didn't have the strength to turn off my heart."

"You're in love with me?" he said, his voice strangely husky.

"I know you won't want to stay here now. Maybe Clare can put you up until—"

"Say it again, Blaze."

"Maybe Clare—"

"Not that, my beautiful idiot, the part about your loving me."

"Taylor, please. Leave me alone. I can't take anymore."

"Blaze, you know how I have always told you who you are? Like Snow White or Heidi or Peter Pan?"

"Yes, but—"

"Do you know who you are right now?"

"A very miserable person."

"You are, my Indian princess, the only woman I have ever loved. You are, I hope, the future Mrs. Taylor Shay. You are the mother of my unborn children. I love you, Blaze Holland, and I will for the rest of my days." He smiled. "The nights won't be too shabby either."

"I don't understand," she said, her voice hardly above a whisper.

"Come sit down and I'll tell you a bedtime story." He led her to the bed and sat her down. "Blaze, the day I met you something clicked inside me. No, make that exploded. There you were pregnant and alone and full of independence and a fiery temper. I couldn't get you off my mind after I dropped you off. I knew I had to see you again. I didn't care that you were having another man's baby. That child was yours and all I knew was I had to be with you and I'd accept that baby, no questions asked."

"But I wasn't pregnant."

"No, and I was so caught up with my thoughts about you that when I saw you at that party I nearly demanded to know what you had done with our child!" He laughed softly at the memory. "I couldn't believe what was happening to me. Then when I didn't rush you into bed that night after we had gone dancing, I knew I was lost forever. I was in love with you, Blaze, and there was no turning back."

"But you said—"

"I know, I know." He nodded. "See, I was frantic. I knew I couldn't just announce I was madly in love with you because I had no idea how you'd feel about it. So, I tested you out and, boy, my worst fears came true. You wanted no part of that stuff and I pretended I thoroughly agreed with you."

"I think I'm getting mad at you."

"You can't, you love me, remember? Anyway, I figured my only prayer was to stick like glue and hope you'd change your mind about husband, hearth, and home. And you did. Oh, Blaze, you love me and those words are the most beautiful I've ever heard."

"Oh, Taylor, I'm not sure I'm believing this."

"You have to because you're stuck with me. It's a wonder I'm still alive though, because Clare threatened to murder me. I told her what I was doing and made her promise not to breath a word of it to you."

"But I made her promise not to tell you how *I* felt."

"Poor Clare. She's probably ready to put a contract out on both of us. Blaze, please, tell me you'll marry me. I want to take the job at NYU because I want my children to know the changing of the seasons and all the beauty that goes with that. Marry me, Blaze."

"Oh, Taylor, yes. Yes, I'll marry you and our babies will play in the snow and smell the flowers in the spring."

"And in all the years we'll share together, I'll never forget the Indian winter that brought you into my life." He kissed her, and when he drew back Blaze was shaken.

"Taylor, I think you should rest now. The doctor said—"

"Let's prove him wrong again, my sweet."

"I love you, Taylor Shay," she said, and moved to meet him in the splendor and ecstasy of the world beyond reality, where they soared together above the stars.

THE EDITOR'S CORNER

With the Olympic Games in Los Angeles much on our minds these past days, we remembered a letter we got last year from Barbara York of Houston, Texas. Barbara gave us a compliment that was truly heart-warming. "If there were an Olympics for category romances," she wrote, "LOVESWEPT would win all the gold medals!"

I don't know about winning them *all* (we're always impressed by the works of talented writers in our competitors' lines). I do know, though, that all our LOVESWEPT authors and staff strive constantly for excellence in our romance publishing program . . . and that we love our work!

And now to the "solid gold" LOVESWEPTS you can expect from us next month.

Joan J. Domning is back with a marvelously evocative romance, **LAHTI'S APPLE**, LOVESWEPT #63. How this romance appeals to the senses. Place, time, sight, sound, tender emotion leap from the pages in this sensitive, yet passionate story of the growing love between heroine Laurian Bryant and hero Keska Lahti. A disillusioned musician, Keska has started an apple orchard and Laurian moves into his world to bring him fully alive. The fragrance of an apple orchard through its seasons . . . the poignant, sometimes melancholy strains of violin and cello are delightfully interwoven with delicate strands of tension between two unforgettable lovers. **LAHTI'S APPLE** stays with you, haunts like a lovely melody.

And what a treat is in store for you in Joan Bramsch's second romance, **A KISS TO MAKE IT BETTER**, LOVESWEPT #64. There's playfulness, joy, humor in

(continued)

this charming love story of Jenny Larsen, a former nurse, and Dr. Jon McCallem. But there is another dimension to this romance—the healing power of love for two sensitive human beings hurt by life's inequities. A simply beautiful story!

Billie Green appeared at one of our teas for LOVE-SWEPT readers not long ago. A lady in the audience got up during the question and answer period with authors and said, "Billie, I love your autobiographical sketches in your books almost as much as I love the books themselves. All I've got to say is thank God for your mother!" There was a big, spontaneous round of applause. Well, that "tetched" quality Billie credits her mother with having passed on to her is present with all its whimsical and enriching power in **THE LAST HERO**, LOVESWEPT #65. Billie's heroine, Toby Baxter, is funny ... but she's also so fragile a personality that you'll find yourself moist of eye and holding your breath. Then Jake Hammond, a dream of a hero—tender, powerful, yet with supreme control—begins to take gentle charge of Toby's life ... to exorcise her demons. Different, dramatic, **THE LAST HERO** is a remarkable love story.

IN A CLASS BY ITSELF, LOVESWEPT #66, by Sandra Brown is aptly titled. It *is* an absolutely spellbinding, one-of-a-kind love story. Dani Quinn is one of Sandra's most lovable heroines ever. And Logan Webster has got to be the most devastatingly attractive man Sandra's ever dreamed up. That walk, that walk, that fabulous walk of Logan's. I guarantee you'll never forget it—nor any of the other elements in this breathtakingly emotional, totally sensual romance. In my judgment, **IN A CLASS BY ITSELF** is Sandra Brown's most delicious, heartwarming love story—in short, my favorite of all her books. You won't want to miss it!

You know, these four LOVESWEPTS *do* have the properties of real gold—shine and brilliance on the surface, the true and "forever" value beneath.

Hope you agree.

Warm regards,

Carolyn Nichols

Carolyn Nichols
   Editor
LOVESWEPT
Bantam Books, Inc.
666 Fifth Avenue
New York, NY 10103